RHONDA GRAFF

ECHO

of

SILENCE

A NOVEL

RIVER GROVE
BOOKS

Published by River Grove Books
Austin, TX
www.rivergrovebooks.com

Distributed by River Grove Books

Design and composition by Greenleaf Book Group and Teresa Muniz
Cover design by Greenleaf Book Group and Teresa Muniz
Cover images used under license from ©Shutterstock.com/reisegraf.ch

Publisher's Cataloging-in-Publication data is available.

Print ISBN: 978-1-63299-314-4

eBook ISBN: 978-1-63299-315-1

First Edition

This novel is not an autobiography. None of the events depicted ever happened to me. There are similarities to places and people I know or have known but all of the characters are 100 percent fiction. I don't know about other writers, as I'm just starting down this journey, but I tend to write about what I know. Thus, any similarities.

Sometimes, she doesn't know the difference between self-loathing and self-pity. They feel so much alike. Both dark. Both cold. Both alone. But they aren't alike. You can keep moving through self-pity. But not with self-loathing.

Chapter 1

THE GOOD LIFE

Summer was magic. School was out. There was swimming at the pool. Staying up late. Sleepovers. It was a time when worries floated away like the lightning bugs flickering in the darkness of dusk. We even got bored—can you imagine? Nothing to do. We'd lay on our backs in the hot shade of a 100-degree Texas sun, chewing a piece of grass—it tasted green and clean. Sometimes, through the branches and leaves, we'd watch clouds drift by pointing out shapes and colors. We had no place to be, and nothing we wanted to do. Nothing we could think to do.

I remember the idea of being bored, but I'm never bored

now. I always have someplace to be. I always have something to do, and most of the time, it's something I don't want to do. I wish, just for a little while, I could be bored again.

My name is Victoria Campbell. I live in Boston, and I work for a well-known Fortune 500 company—one you would recognize if I told you the name. I make a lot of money, which, frankly, doesn't matter to me one way or the other. Money has never been the key to my motivation. Basically, I'm a people pleaser by nature. And I've always felt the need to be in the top of my class, among the A+ group. I was the kid who always read the most books, did extra work, and had the highest scores on tests.

Why the need to be the best? I'm not really sure. As far back as I can remember, I felt an obligation to accomplish so that my parents, my grandparents, everyone would be proud. My family didn't ask this of me; in fact, it was quite the opposite. I was pampered and indulged. I hate to admit it, but I was very spoiled.

Outwardly, I know I seemed 100% normal. I had lots of friends, joined all the right school organizations, had a boyfriend, went to prom, hung out with the "in" crowd. I enjoyed all that, but I carried self-doubt with me all the time. I couldn't imagine failing. But, let's face it. We all fail. With time, I realized that, but my motivation hasn't changed. I still need to be the best at whatever I do.

But enough about then. Now, I live in an upscale neighborhood in downtown Boston, and by upscale, I mean most expensive. I own a brownstone. Brownstones are wonderful buildings. Most were built in the mid to late 1800s or early 1900s. Mine was built in 1889, a three-story walkup. The stairs keep us all in shape. It sits in a parallel row of similar brownstones on Commonwealth Avenue E.

All of the brownstones in this neighborhood are immaculately maintained with seasonal landscaping in each "yard" and old trees and bushes lining the sidewalks. Over the years, the bricks have erupted like land after an earth-quake—uneven, jagged—tripping hazards if you aren't careful. The exterior of the buildings isn't usually brown but more often red-brick with black, wrought iron hand-rails, fences, and gates.

My building has four units. I live in the fourth unit at the top of the building—Number 4. I lease the other three units.

My unit has 2,500 square feet. Measured by the small-town standards where I grew up, that equates to about 10,000 square feet in Boston. I remodeled it before I moved in two years ago. I moved here from San Francisco. I did very well there too, but my current company really pressed the hard sell—more money, more benefits, and, most significantly, more recognition. And I've always loved Boston, so I moved from the sunshine to the snow.

I hired a high-end and very expensive decorator to help me design and furnish the space. Against his advice, I insisted we add a lot of color. My bedroom is a very light shade of green—Barely Mint, he called it. The living room is orange—I know! It's called Maui Sunset, which *paints* the picture, I think—pun intended. The kitchen is yellow, not bright, pale with white trim. The dining room opening into the living room is white but with Maui Sunset trim. The two extra bedrooms are gray with white trim, clean.

I love linens. I splurged on everything—sheets, duvet covers, pillows. Luxurious and, like the paint, colorful. Different patterns and colors—deep purples, reds, greens, blues, and oranges. Actually, all the linens, even the bath and kitchen towels, are overexaggerated with these colors. I know it all sounds unappealing, but somehow the decorator pulled it all together. Even when "colorless" people see my home, I think they begrudgingly like it—it's warm and welcoming. At least that's my hope.

The furniture is "modern rustic"—decorator's term, not mine. Basically, it means the wood is rough, the metal is silver, the surfaces are black granite, and there's a lot of glass. He conceded to my request for colors, so I gave him more free rein with the rest of the place.

My kitchen is a gourmet chef's dream. Stainless steel industrial side by side refrigerator-freezer. Gas range with double ovens and warming drawers. Two dishwashers. Double sinks. Two walk-in pantries. Mounted convection microwave. Prep island stocked with every gizmo and gadget Sur la Table and Williams Sonoma sell. Extravagant—especially for someone who doesn't cook.

I have an exercise room, a study, a landscaped terrace at the back of the building with an outdoor kitchen, a pizza oven, and seating for twelve.

I have a basement with two parking spaces for me and

one for each of my tenants. Parking spots in Boston are an endangered species. My tenants pay extra to use them.

I own a Mercedes, a Range Rover, and a Porsche. The Porsche is over the top—I know. I can justify the Mercedes, which I need for getting around town, and the Range Rover for weekends out, but the Porsche. Well, there's no justification. It's a 2018, white 911 coupe with brown leather interior. It's beautiful. I don't drive much, though. I'm actually a very good driver, but the streets are narrow and traffic is tight in Boston. I can't get used to it. I have a driver, Jim. He picks me up for work each morning at five-thirty and is there when I leave, whatever time that is. The extra work time in the car is a plus. And Jim and I have become friends. He lives in Brookline in another building I own. He keeps the Mercedes at his place.

Jim's wife, Julie, is a personal chef. She makes most of my meals, and if I have parties, she caters them. She's fairly well known in the culinary circle, but that's not why I hired her. The fact is her food is amazing.

I could go on, but you've heard enough and you get the picture anyway.

Like I said, I make a lot of money.

I'm thirty-eight. I graduated from The University of Texas in Austin with a degree in finance and then went back and finished my master's and PhD in economics there.

I started working full-time at twenty-three. I've been recruited away from six different jobs since then, always for more pay, more benefits, more stock options, and more pressure. I'm going to stay where I am now to see how high up the corporate ladder I can go.

I'm not married. I've had a few boyfriends over the years, but past experiences hold me back. My therapist says I've built this impenetrable barrier to keep people at bay. Not my family, of course. When she talks about "people," she really means men. I think she's probably right, but all the talk in the world hasn't changed it. She says to give it more time.

My parents and my three siblings live in Texas, where I grew up. William, Annie, and Christopher; they're all married. Something my mother desperately wants for me.

I love my family very much. I'm very close to all of them, especially Will. But I don't go home often. Thank God for FaceTime and email.

My parents have been married forty-five years, and they are still so kind to each other. I'm very proud of them for that. Being kind to someone for that long—well, I just can't imagine. But I'm glad for them and for all of us. My dad is retired now and does a lot of fishing. Mom likes fishing too. They spend days at a time working those rods and reels. Before retiring, my dad owned the local John Deere dealership. He sold it several years ago and did very well. When I was growing up, my mom was a dental hygienist, but she quit working when I was a senior in high school.

Five years ago, I bought a house on Lake Lyndon B. Johnson, otherwise known as Lake LBJ, near Marble Falls. It's beautiful. I told my family it was a good investment, which it is. The house is big enough to sleep everyone, and it has a guesthouse out back with two extra bedrooms and a small kitchen. And it sits right on the lake. LBJ is a constant level lake, so it's prime real estate.

My real goal in buying the house was to move family holidays away from the ranch. I love the ranch, but it's hard for me to go there. Don't get me wrong; it was a wonderful place to grow up, and it still holds a big piece of my heart. But after college and all that happened, I never had the courage to go back and face the gossip of a small town. I missed my friends, but I didn't want to talk to them either. Too much time, too much pain, too many memories.

For the past five years, we've celebrated the 4th of July, Easter, Thanksgiving, and Christmas at LBJ. I know my family wants to be at the ranch, but they love me, so we meet at the lake.

Other than a very out-of-the-ordinary trip, those holidays are the only times I go to Texas. My oldest brother, Will, makes it a point to come see me at least twice a year wherever I live. I get the feeling he is the designated guardian to check out my life and make sure I'm doing well. After he married Susie, they both visit. We always have wonderful times.

Dad and Mom have come to visit in each city where I've lived. Before San Francisco, I lived in Denver. They loved Denver and came often. They both ski and hike so we spent weekends in the mountains. Denver, by far, has been their favorite city. They haven't made it to Boston, though.

Chapter 2

ALL WORK

"Victoria, they need you in conference room ten."

That's my assistant, Margaret. She's a pushy sort, but that's actually good for me. Sometimes I just stop, and Margaret winds me up and gets me going again.

"Okay, I'm on my way. I thought the meeting didn't start until ten."

"If you would keep up with emails, you'd know Liam changed it to nine-thirty."

See what I mean. Pushy.

I grab my coffee, my laptop, and the folder prepared by Liam's secretary for the meeting. It's a juggling act, but I

make it to the elevator and punch the up arrow to conference room ten.

I walk in before the meeting starts, but I wouldn't care if
it had. This isn't my project. I'm just a supporting character,
and a minor one at that. But I do like Liam, so I told him I
would help. I'll monitor the progress of the product when
it's introduced into the market, but no late-night design or
overall strategy sessions for me.

Liam coughs slightly, a ploy to get the attention of the
room.

"Thanks, guys, for coming a little early. I want to introduce the team. Some of you might already know each other,
but I still think this is a good way to start. Actually, let's all
introduce ourselves. I'm Liam, project head."

He grins. We all know who he is and that he heads the
team.

Liam turns to the woman to his left. "You next, Lu."

"I'm Lu Chang. I'm in charge of finance."

The introductions continue—Bill in charge of product design and prototype. Carolyn in charge of marketing.
Jam—yes that's really his name—in charge of distribution.
And so it goes until all ten people have introduced themselves. I really hate these role calls, but Liam looks at me
with no intention of giving me a pass.

"Victoria, product review," I mumble.

So—I'll bet you thought I'd speak right up, confident and
sure. And that's fair. I've led you to believe that's who I am—
confident and sure. Except I'm not. I'm shy, timid and, quite

frankly, the mouse in the room. You don't expect people like me to have my job or make the money I do. I don't fit into the outgoing corporate mold. I try my best not to attend client lunches or dinners or anything like that. I don't party after hours with my coworkers. I avoid office events, and I go home as soon as possible. I don't socialize. So how do I do it? Get the great jobs and make the money? Well, I'm very smart.

And I work really, really hard. I'm at the office by six every morning. When Jim picks me up at five-thirty, he has my Starbucks ready. Unless there's a lunch I can't dodge, I eat at my desk. Margaret gets it for me. Usually potato soup and ham and Swiss on whole wheat. Iced tea all day long. Can take the girl out of Texas, but she needs her iced tea!

I never leave before seven-thirty in the evening, even if I have a dinner appointment I can't avoid (appointment, not date). Those start at eight and usually don't end until ten o'clock. I hate them. Even without dinners and more often than not, I don't get back home until ten-thirty or eleven. I allow myself one hour that's all mine. I usually shower, listen to music, sometimes read—but I read so much for work, it's not often.

And then I begin two to three hours of work—reports, market analysis, financials, legal contracts—it's never-ending. But that's who I am. And I'm surely not going to let anyone outwork me.

Around two or so, I try to sleep. I'm ashamed to admit it, but I've resorted to drugs. I have to sleep, and it never comes without meds. Before you judge, just know I've tried everything—chamomile tea, melatonin, valerian root, white noise, massage, meditation. I've seen chiropractors, hypnotists, acupuncturists, psychics, and finally—real doctors. That's how I got the drugs. Anyway, after a few hours of sleep, I start all over.

Never bored. Just exhausted.

"Victoria, you aren't paying attention," Liam scolds me.

"What? Sorry. Did you ask me something?"

You can hear the snickering in the room. Just another reason I don't like the team approach. It's like being back in grade school. Everyone is so immature.

"Yes. I asked if you can start product review if we roll out in three months."

"Wow, you think you will be ready by then?"

"That's the goal."

Liam's frustrated with me. I wish he weren't. It just makes me nervous and anxious.

"I have a few of my own project deadlines around that time."

"I know. That's why I asked."

He's super frustrated.

"I'll make it work. Don't worry."

The people pleaser. That's me. It will almost kill me, but I'll get it done. I don't want to disappoint.

"I know it will be tough, but we know what a machine you are!"

He's smiling now. A machine. Really. That's—insulting. But I smile back.

"Well, I don't want to let down the team." Internal grimace.

"Great. Okay, let's move on to marketing."

I'm dismissed. Thankfully.

The meeting goes through lunch so we order in. Sushi. I just don't get sushi. Everyone says they love it. But do they really? Hardcore, it's just raw fish. Anyway, I pretend to like it and order the California rolls. Mostly, I just pick out the avocado and rice.

About one-thirty, it's finally over. As I get up to leave, Liam comes over and asks me to wait until the others have gone. It's a bit unnerving.

"Vic, I'm sorry if I came off like a jerk earlier."

When did he start calling me Vic? I hate it.

"Don't worry about it." People pleaser. "I was just daydreaming. I'm sorry I wasn't more attentive."

"Well, I just wanted to apologize anyway. I'm really glad you agreed to join the team. I know how busy you are. I appreciate it."

What's with the apologies?

"It's not a problem. I'm glad I can contribute." Liar.

"Hey, since I know how much you work, I thought you might like to take a break sometime and go to dinner or something."

Oh God! Please do not tell me he is asking me out on a date. Last thing I want, especially as we're working together.

"Sure. Sure. That sounds good. Sometime." Stall. I'm not going to dinner with Liam.

"So I know you're a Red Sox fan. They play the Rangers this weekend. Saturday. A Texas team."

That grin again. Damn, I do love baseball and what a great game. Could I do it? Just be normal, casual?

"That actually sounds great." Did I just say yes? "I'm surprised you remembered I like baseball. I barely mentioned it."

"I pay attention." Still grinning. "I'll pick you up about one o'clock. The game starts at two."

"I'll just meet you there, at the gate." Stall again.

"Riding together is half the fun. I'd really like to pick you up."

"Well—okay. Do you have my address?"

"Of course. Firm directory, remember?"

Yes, I remember, but it's weird he looked it up. Is it creepy?

"Right. Okay, I'll see you Saturday."

"You'll see me around here, too."

What is with that constant grin? It's goofy and silly, two things I am not.

"Yes, guess you will."

I head for the door. I feel the panic coming.

"Okay, then."

He heads back to the conference table to gather papers. I barely make it to the bathroom, sink to my knees. It starts, full-on. Racing heart—but not a heart attack. I know that. My therapist and I have been through it many times. Sweating. Dry mouth. Nausea. Then bubbling saliva. Tunnel vision. All alone.

I don't have my purse. No Xanax. Just need to gut it out.
Like the first time.

Chapter 3

SLOW FADE

Nineteen years ago, October

I wake up slowly. For just a minute I forget. I wish I'd never remember. But I do. I get up slowly. Turn so I'm sitting before standing. Every muscle in my body is screaming. Throbbing pain, dull pain, aching pain—just pain. I get up and move to my sink. There are two in the dorm room. One for Sally Ann and one for me. Two beds on either side of the room, matching desks, two closets, and two sinks. My dorm is women only, so we have a community bath with lots of showers—no tubs. Too bad. Soaking in a hot bath would help.

I don't want to wake Sally Ann. She's from a small town in West Virginia. She's had trouble adjusting to college already. She'd freak if she saw me now. I know, without looking, there's blood on my face. It feels like my lip might be swollen. I make it to the sink and, as quietly as I can, turn on the water. I clean my face without looking in the mirror. Only after I'm finished do I look.

It's not as bad as I thought. Cut above my right eyebrow, slightly swollen lip. I can manage this. Little Band-Aid and some lip gloss. I find the Advil and take four. I'll take four more in a few hours.

I don't stop to count the bruises. I know how to cover them up.

I creep back to bed and wait for the Advil to kick in. I have some Vicodin, but I don't use it. I use that only when it's really bad.

It's four a.m., and I can't sleep. I try to block out what happened, but I can't. He told me to meet him at the corner of Sixth and Lavaca at eight o'clock sharp. I took a cab. Paid with his money.

I close my eyes and I'm there again.

Sixth Street is getting revved up. Bars open. Music playing—loud. People crowding the street. Everyone laughing, singing, drinking, happy. No one notices me.

He pulls to the curb and motions for me to get in. I do. He reaches over and pulls my face to his, kissing me gently.

"Hey, Vic, darling. It's so good to see you."

"You too." I mean it. I smile. My body hums being this close to him.

"Ready to go?"

"Yes! How about you?"

"Always."

He laughs and drives. I sit next to him, stroking his neck. He likes this. I know. He glances at me and smiles. Sometimes he touches my hair or my face. But that's all. We don't talk.

We drive for about thirty minutes to a house he rents. We pull into the driveway. I duck until the garage door closes. We both get out. I wait for him. He comes to me and pushes me, hard, against the car. And it starts.

Tangled together, we go through the garage door into the house. That's as far as we get. We have to stop. He takes off my shirt; I'm not wearing a bra. He touches my nipples, pulls them. It hurts. Kind of. He takes off his shirt. I used to love his chest. I reach up to touch him. I know that's what he wants.

He pushes me down on the kitchen floor. It's tile—hard and cold, but I don't feel it.

He slides down my body. He looks up at me, grinning. He knows he's in control.

"Are you ready, baby?"

"Yes," I barely whisper. I'm trembling. My legs shake. I just want him to start.

"How do you ask?"

"Please."

I hold my breath and close my eyes.

My hips reach up to him. I can't help it. Deeper, stronger. I feel the building, almost to the edge. He pulls back.

He does that often. Thinks it's funny. He smiles. "I love you."

"I love you, too."

He starts again. I break over the edge and fall into spasms, wave after wave of oblivion.

He quickly moves into me while I'm still surfing, and before I'm finished, he starts again. This time we surf together and break the waves at the same time. I pull him to me as close as I can, and we rock. I hope it lasts.

And then it's over.

We both lie back. I know what comes next. Was it worth it? It's like an addiction. You know it's killing you, but you love the high.

I rest on the tile, waiting. Knowing. It's okay, I tell myself. This is just his thing. It's not bad—just different.

He picks me up and carries me. I try to just ride the waves. He throws me on the bed and falls on top of me. He squeezes my arms, up high, on the biceps.

I used to say things like, "Baby, you're hurting me," or "Please don't do that." It only made it worse. Now I don't talk unless he tells me what to say.

"I know you fuck other men." First slap, carefully placed. Still hurts. I try not to move.

"You need to be punished. I'm sorry I always have to do this. I wish you wouldn't fuck other men. Then I wouldn't have to."

My cue. "Baby, you know I don't. You just get these ideas in your head. They aren't true."

Second slap. This is where I start the slow fade.

"Don't lie to me. I know what you do. You think I don't, but I do. I have people watching you. They tell me. Did you know that?"

The script is different, but the theme's the same.

"No, I didn't, but whatever you've heard, it's not true."

I'm supposed to sound pitiful. I don't have to pretend.

He rolls me over. Right in—no warm-up. No warmth. It doesn't hurt much. Not anymore. I moan. He thinks I'm turned on.

He turns me back to face him. Complete fade. I'm gone.

When he's finished, he cries. He tells me how sorry he is. I believe him. I know he is sorry. I kiss his tears.

It's eleven-thirty. I want to go home, and he wants me to go. We drive back to Sixth Street. He hands me two hundred dollars.

"For the cab—and stuff."

"Thanks. I love you."

I kiss him and open the door. As I'm about to shut it, he says, "Vic." I look in the car, "I love you, too."

"I know." I smile.

I grab a cab, and by midnight, Cinderella is back home, and the carriage is a pumpkin again.

Chapter 4

REGRET

After that meeting, I bump into Liam every day, even though I do my best to avoid him. How does it keep happening? Is he stalking me? Of course not. I'm just paranoid. I wish I could take back my agreement to the Saturday game.

On Friday morning, we ride the elevator together. Seems he comes in early too. I never noticed that before. It's an opening, though.

"Um, Liam, hey, about tomorrow." I want out of it. "I think you should invite someone else to the game."

"What? Why? You said you wanted to go." Is he upset?

"I did, I mean, I do, but I just have so much work. You

know how it is. I've got five projects of my own, and I'm helping you and John Stanford with his new project."

"What? You're helping John Stanford? Why? What's his project?"

Why does he care? He's definitely upset. He almost sounds jealous. This can't be possible, can it? He doesn't even know me, not really. This is crazy.

"He asked about a month ago. I'm just consulting. I'm not even an official team member."

"You should have told me when I asked you to join my team."

He looks away from me. Is he pouting?

"Honestly, Liam. I don't think it's a big deal. I can get it all done."

He whips back around, glaring at me.

"But you can't go to the game."

Wow! Who is this guy? Not the nice guy, for sure.

"Obviously, I *could* go, but—"

"Then, it's still on. You can go." Now he smiles.

I'm stunned. What just happened? The elevator door opens on the fifth floor, my floor. I get out. I don't respond.

"I'll see you at one. Have a great day. TGIF, right?"

"Right."

I reach in my purse for the bottle.

I make it through work. Margaret is unbearable. Relentless. She pushes and pushes until I want to scream. But I don't. At six-thirty, she checks in for the last time. Finally. Thankfully.

"Are you sure you don't need me to stay, Victoria?"

"Margaret, good God! It's Friday evening. Go home to your family. I'm fine. I'm good."

"Well, what about you? You need to knock off too. You need rest."

"I'll leave soon. I just want to finish the McKenzie report. I'm halfway through. If I stop now, I'll just have to start over."

"Okay, promise? I worry about you. All you do is work."

I get up and give her a hug. She's a really good person and has been caring and supportive of my quirks since I got here. I often remind myself how lucky I am that she works with me.

"I promise. And I do not always work. In fact, I'm going to the Red Sox game tomorrow."

"Really?" I shouldn't have told her. "That's amazing! I'm so glad. Who are you going with?"

Why did I start this? Margaret always feels sorry for me, and, as much as I know she has my best interest at heart, I'm tired of it. Actually, when it comes down to it, I'm tired of feeling sorry for myself.

"Umm, Liam."

"Like our Liam? Liam Nelson?"

And she's off.

"Well, the Liam Nelson that works here, yes."

Is she crying?

"I'm so glad!"

She hugs me again.

"Margaret, get a grip. It's a baseball game, for God's sake. It's not a big deal."

"Well . . . we'll see. I want a complete report Monday." Instant flush. What does she think is going to happen?

"Okay, okay but, believe me, there won't be anything to report. Now, please go home so I can finish."

I go back to my desk.

"Alright. I'm going." Sigh. "Victoria."

"Yes?"

"You deserve happiness, you know?"

She's out the door. I swivel my chair and watch the sunset. I look back and remember all that happened. I know it wasn't my fault. I know I was a victim, but there's still guilt. Did I do something to make it happen? Maybe I'm being punished. Do I deserve happiness? I'm not so sure. I close my eyes.

Chapter 5

IN THE BEGINNING

Nineteen years ago, August.

I wasn't expecting it. The first time I saw him. My high school boyfriend and I broke up the early part of my freshman year. Even though it had been almost a year, I was still hurting, not ready to try again.

He commanded the room. All eyes on him. Total attention from the crowd. From me too. I felt like he was speaking only to me. Probably everyone felt that way.

What was it about him? Of course, he was handsome.

Tall, dark hair, blue eyes. Athletic, strong. I found out later he played soccer.

But it was more than looks. His voice was low, but so clear, you could hear every word he said, even at the back of the room where I sat. He looked at us—really looked around the room as he talked. No notes, no fumbling. An intimate conversation.

"As we go through this class on Revelations, my goal is to help you find your own revelation. I know that sounds corny, but I don't want the class to be just about the material we cover. I want it to be about personal growth. We'll grow together. Every time I teach this class, I grow too. We get what we give, right?"

Heads nodding.

I almost passed on this class. It wasn't like I needed it. Taking eighteen hours was crushing, but I'd heard his class was amazing. They were right. I was amazed.

He gave us reading assignments from the course book he wrote, *A Personal Revelation*, and selected chapters of the Bible for background and context. And then, class was over.

I fumbled for my backpack, ready to leave. When I looked up, he was standing beside me. I startled.

"I noticed you sitting by yourself here at the back of the room. Don't like people?"

I didn't respond. Just looked at him.

"So, do you like people or not?" He was teasing me.

"Yes, I like people. I was late. I didn't want to bother anyone."

"Okay. I'll accept that. Next time, come join the group—even if you bother someone." Dazzling smile. I had to look away. I couldn't even make eye contact. I tried to hurry up and finish what I was doing and get out of the room.

"I will. Thanks."

The class was leaving. People stared at us. It was uncomfortable.

"Guess I'd better go."

"Why did you sign up for this class?"

I bit my lower lip. Nervous habit.

"Umm, someone recommended it. It sounded interesting."

"Are you a religious person?"

Am I?

"I'm not sure what you mean by religious. I believe in God. I'm still processing the rest."

He laughed. I felt foolish.

"Honest. Good. I like that. I believe in God too. Obviously. But I'm further along in the process. Maybe I can help you."

"Well, that's one of the reasons I'm taking this class."

The classroom was empty and very uncomfortable.

"I know."

What does he know?

"I'd like to help you more if I can. I believe God calls me to certain people for His purpose. I think He called me to you."

Such bullshit. What a line.

"I don't know what to say. What do you mean by 'help me?'"

"We could meet once or twice a week for lunch or something and talk. You can tell me what you are 'processing,' and I'll tell you what I think. Give you some different scripture to study. Maybe suggest some books for you."

On one hand, who wouldn't want to spend time with this guy? But it didn't feel right. Actually, it felt wrong.

"Do you do this kind of thing often? I mean, I'm in your class."

He laughed again.

"No. God doesn't call that often. And, it doesn't matter that you're in my class. You're taking this pass-fail anyway, right? I'm sure you'll pass."

How did he know that? And God called him. Really?!

"I don't think your other students would see it that way."

"Why do you care so much about what other people think? I don't."

"I just do."

I looked down. He lifted my chin. His touch was electric. I felt it go to my toes.

"This time, don't. Trust God's hand in this. All things to His purpose. Let's meet tomorrow for lunch and see how you feel after that."

I wish he would stop touching me. I can't think.

"Okay, we can try it tomorrow and see, I guess."

No harm, no foul. He stepped back.

"I'll meet you here, and we can decide where to go. What time?"

Is this okay? I'm still not sure. Anyway, after tomorrow I don't have to go again.

"I have classes until three."

"So let's meet at three-thirty and do late lunch, early dinner."

"Okay. But I really have to go now. I have another class in thirty minutes."

"Sure." Dazzling smile again. "I'm sorry I kept you so long. I just know when God calls, I have to answer. I'll see you tomorrow. Blessings to you, Victoria."

He seemed genuinely interested in helping me.

"Don't worry about it, and, uh, thanks."

As I left, I realized he knew my name. But I never told him.

Chapter 6

JUST LUNCH

Nineteen Years Ago, August.

I met him in the classroom. He was so charming—worldly. He wore white linen pants and a pale blue, button-down shirt—maybe linen too, and sandals. He definitely didn't look the part of a typical college professor.

He was so relaxed, and I was a wreck. I hadn't slept much the night before. In my heart, I knew seeing him outside of class wasn't a good idea. But he was magnetic. A force. And so, I was at his classroom at three-thirty, as planned.

What was I wearing? I chose my clothes carefully, even

if it didn't look like it. Faded jeans and a pearl snap western shirt. Flip flops, my hair in a messy bun. Big gold hoop earrings. No need to impress, right? This was a lunch about philosophy.

You know that smile people have when they see someone they really like? Like there's no one else they want to see and nothing they wanted to do except be with that person? That's the look he gave me when I walked into his classroom. It was unnerving. It totally freaked me out. I couldn't make eye contact.

"Hey, I'm so glad you're here. I've been waiting to see you all day, really since yesterday."

I wasn't sure how to respond.

"Well, I'm here now." Stammering. "Where would you like to go eat?"

"I thought we could go to Mario's."

As in Mario's across town? Only the best Italian restaurant in the city. Totally upscale. I'd never been there. Not many college students had been there; it wasn't in the price range for most of us.

"I kind of thought we'd walk to a place close to campus. Anyway, I'm not dressed for Mario's."

"Are you kidding? You look amazing. It doesn't matter who else is there, you'll be the most gorgeous woman in the place. And, anyway, I know the owner, so believe me, you'll be fine."

I didn't believe him, but I was flattered.

"I really feel underdressed."

"Victoria, like I told you yesterday, you need to stop worrying about what other people think."

As he talked, he turned me toward the door, took my hand, and led me out of the building.

It was surreal. I don't know now why I didn't stop and insist we stay near campus. I guess he was just so beautiful. Being with him made me feel beautiful too. So I went with him—nervous and scared but excited, too.

"You know, before we start processing God together, we should probably know each other better, don't you think?"

Did I think? I didn't know what to think. My arm felt like it was burning where he touched me. I could barely breathe. And, I was scared. I know now that was what I was feeling. But fear was overshadowed by his force, his attention.

"Okay, sure, I guess. What do you want to know?"

"Everything. I want to know everything about you. Where you were born. About your family. Do you have siblings? What do you do for fun? About your friends. Do you have a boyfriend?"

The last question, delivered casually, hung in the air. He waited for my answer.

We'd reached the faculty parking lot. He clicked his key fob and a black Jeep Cherokee answered. He opened my door. I got in and put my purse on the floorboard. He went around on the other side of the Jeep and got in the driver's seat and started the engine. Before he backed out, he turned toward me.

"So? Tell me about Victoria."

"I don't have a boyfriend." He turned around and started backing out of the parking space.

"Why not?" We pulled out onto Guadalupe.

"Well, just not interested right now, I guess."

"You've got to be kidding. An amazing woman like you and no boyfriend?"

Did he really say that? Totally inappropriate. I knew he was older than me—a lot older. It felt off. And we were supposed to talk about God. Still, it was exciting. No man had ever said anything like that to me. In fact, to that point in my life, I'd only dated boys.

I didn't respond at first. He waited. We drove.

"I'm not sure we're clear here. I know I'm not beautiful. Wholesome, girl-back-home cute, maybe. That's it."

"No, you're wrong, Victoria. You don't see it, but everyone else does. You don't see how the men in class watch you."

I didn't know how to respond. Time to change the subject.

"Um, well anyway, to be truthful, I did have a boyfriend. We broke up about a year ago. We'd been dating since we were juniors in high school. I guess my heart is still broken." I said it jokingly, but it was truer than I cared to admit. It may not have been a long-term deal, but breaking up was still painful. I'd lost some of my self-confidence, and it made me weary of any new relationship.

He reached across the seat and put his hand on mine.

"Don't worry. God will send you a special man who will appreciate and care for you. Someone to love you more than you can even imagine. I don't know about the old boyfriend, but my guess is he'll be very sorry one day."

I wanted someone to say those things to me. I'd lost my self-confidence after the breakup. He'd found my underbelly, my weakest spot. I forgot about being scared or the wrong-ness of what he said. The dance had begun. I was caught in the quicksand and didn't even know it.

During lunch (he knew the owner and got us a private table), I told him about my life. He asked questions and I answered. The food was incredible but I barely ate. Actually, I drank—glass after glass of very expensive wine.

It was only later—five hours later—after he dropped me off that I realized he didn't talk about himself at all. We talked about me, school, music, and what was happening in Austin . . . at least that's what I remember. And we certainly did not work on processing my beliefs.

The more I drank, the more I was drawn to him. I touched his arm, his hand, and, I think, even his face. He touched my elbow, my knee, my hair. We moved our chairs closer to each other. I told him I thought he was beautiful. He laughed again. He laughed at me a lot. It was endearing back then.

"No, Vic. You really and truly are beautiful. I don't know why you can't see it. Frankly, I can't believe I'm sitting here with you. I'm older than you, you know. You could have your pick of any of those young guys."

That was the first time he called me Vic.

He leaned in and kissed me. It was magic. I felt warm and whole. That day, it was only the one kiss. He was so smart.

He knew just how to set the stage so I would put my fears aside and start trusting him. I see that now. But at the time, I thought he was a gentleman.

We agreed to meet the next day after classes, and from the time he left me back on campus, I waited for morning.

Chapter 7

TAKE ME OUT TO THE BALL GAME

It's only a baseball game—which I love. I told myself this all morning. I didn't eat lunch. My stomach rolled. No way I'm putting anything in it. By twelve-thirty, I'm basically sick. Liam knocked on the door at one on the dot. Punctual.

"Hey, you ready? You look great!"

Jeans, my old Rangers jersey, game cap, and tennis shoes. I wore the cap because when you have short hair like mine, and you sweat, it's better to cover it up. Definitely not great.

"Thanks, I guess. I didn't dress to impress." That sounded

bitchy. "I'm sorry. It's just—well—I don't think of this as great, but anyway, yes, I'm ready. Let's go."

We walked to the elevator. It was awkward. I didn't have a thing to say to him. I wanted to turn around and go back home.

"So, you're not rooting for the hometown team?"

"Are you even kidding? I'm from Texas. That's my home!"

"Whoa! Didn't mean to offend. So, how about a bet on the game?"

"I don't know. I don't bet. I always lose."

"Well, if you're afraid Texas won't win—"

"Okay, okay. What do you want to bet?"

The elevator door opened. At least the tension had cleared a bit. Maybe I could do this.

"A real live date—like with dinner and wine and dessert—the works. That's what I want. Now you pick what you want."

I already hated where this was going. Geez, always the date thing with men. He seemed so genuine, though. What harm in playing along?

"How about ice cream every afternoon for a week, my choice." Where did that come from?

He laughed—a deep, soulful laugh. I kind of liked it. I relaxed a bit. I even thought I might have fun.

"Okay, you're on. You crack me up! Ice cream. Ha!"

We walked outside and down the steps. He parked at the curb. He opened the door for me. I kind of liked that too. I'm always a sucker for chivalry. Some women find it offensive when men open doors or pull out chairs, but that's how I was raised. That's what my daddy and my brother did. It felt a bit like home.

"What's wrong with ice cream? It's more original than a date!"

"Yeah, it's different. But I'm gonna win, so you'll have to save it for another bet."

"And just why do you think that? The Rangers are killing it this year."

"Right, they have been but (a), they're not at home, (b), Hamilton and Kinsler are injured, and (c), Munoz is suspended."

Smug smile, twinkle in his eyes. Obviously, I haven't been keeping up this season.

"What? No comeback?"

"Well, shit, it looks like we're going to dinner."

That laugh again. I grinned and looked out the window. Maybe it would be alright.

The Rangers lost 19 to 17. Reluctantly, I admit I had fun. We might have flirted. It felt okay. I ate a hot dog and drank a beer. Maybe that's progress.

Back at my door.

"So, about that date."

"Don't rub it in. I really wanted that ice cream!"

"A bet's a bet. Do you want to pick when and where or do you want me to?"

"Liam, look, we're both so busy at work—I'm already behind just taking this afternoon off. I don't see how either of us have time."

He leaned in and kissed me. Gently, barely a touch. Nice.

"Okay then, I pick. Friday evening at seven. I'll surprise you, and I'll pick you up here—not at work."

"I just don't know if I can."

"I won. You have to."

He kissed me again. Still just a brush. Not too scary.

"Okay—a bet's a bet."

He waved and walked to the elevator.

I worked the rest of the weekend and was back at the office the usual time Monday morning. I thought about him off and on. Admittedly, it was a bit distracting, but I have great focus.

Monday at noon, Margaret brought my lunch.

"You have a package. Looks like one of those meal deal things."

"What? Like a meal kit? I didn't order that."

"I'm not sure what it is. But here, open it."

The return address gave nothing away.

"Well, let's hope it's not a bomb!"

"Now why would you even say something like that?" She actually put her hands on her hips and frowned at me.

"Just kidding."

"Not funny."

"Okay, fine."

I opened the package. Two gallons of Blue Bell Homemade Vanilla, from Brenham, Texas.

"Well, what is it?"

"Ice cream."

Chapter 8

WINNER, WINNER CHICKEN DINNER

It seemed the work week flew by, and I didn't hate it. I got a package with different Blue Bell ice cream every day. Tuesday—Strawberry, Wednesday—Cookies 'n Cream, Thursday—Mint Chocolate Chip, and Friday—Chocolate, my favorite.

News of the ice cream deliveries spread through the office. I finally sent a group email to everyone explaining about the bet and inviting anyone with a spoon to come by and share. I wanted to squash any rumors of a budding romance. I'm not sure it worked. Office gossip has a life of its own.

That type of gesture isn't like me at all, but what the heck? I couldn't eat all that ice cream myself.

Surprisingly, at least to me, lots of people came by, spoon in hand when they heard the latest delivery arrived. I finally told Margaret to get a scoop and paper bowls so we could actually serve the stuff.

Liam came too. On Monday, I thanked him and we both laughed about it.

"You know you didn't need to do this. I lost the bet, remember?"

"Yeah, I know, but I thought it might make you happy."

I smiled. He seemed so sincere.

"Well, to tell you the truth, it does. Ice cream is my weakness. Want to try some?"

"I've never tasted Blue Bell. Let's see if it's as good as the ads say."

"Oh, it is!"

"So about the bet. I did win."

"Okay, dinner it is. Friday, right? Where do you want to go?"

"What?! No fight, no complaining?"

"Nope. You won, and besides, you're kind of growing on me."

"Be still my heart—did you, Victoria Jean Campbell just say you LIKE me?"

He knows my middle name. That's odd. Did I tell him what it was?

"No, I did not say I like you. I said you are growing on me."

"Well, if it doesn't mean you like me, what does it mean?"

"It means I can tolerate you being around."

I ate another spoonful of ice cream. It felt silly, flirting. I don't really know how to flirt. Even when I was younger, I wasn't a giggling girly-girl. With my brothers, being boy-crazy wasn't an option. And with all that happened, well—flirting just wasn't an option much anymore either.

But . . . what's a girl to do? I was actually starting to enjoy Liam. Hated to admit it to myself, and of course, I was terrified.

"Good to know. Hopefully I can drag that 'tolerate' up the scale to 'like' before dinner is over."

"You know, we could bet on that! I'd love another week of ice cream."

"Oh, I don't think you really want to bet again. You don't have a winning record, and besides, it's a given I would win."

"Oh really?"

"Really."

I blushed.

Finally, Friday came. For the first time since I could remember, I was excited about something. I didn't expect to feel that way. I was totally off my game, and don't think Margaret didn't notice! She smiled at me all day like she was my fairy godmother, and I was going to the ball. She covered my slipups and kept most of my work at bay.

At four o'clock, she finally said, "Just go home. Take a long bath. Relax. Maybe drink a glass of wine. You need to loosen up and try to act normal."

"Gee, thanks, Mags. You are so supportive."

She and I had spent more time than I had to spare during the week talking about the dinner. We went over what I should wear—Margaret voted for something new. I said no. She wanted to select shoes, jewelry, and how to wear my hair. I said no.

We were both wound tight. But, when she suggested it, I left.

"You know I do support you. I just want you to have fun."

"I know, and you want me to fall madly in love." Always the goal for both Margaret and my mother.

"Of course. That, too. But, seriously, Victoria, give Liam a chance. He's a really great guy."

"I will. I promise." What are the odds anyway? Frankly, I'd given up on having any kind of meaningful relationship. I'm just too wary, too suspicious, too careful. And, I don't think I'm that much fun, either. As time has passed, work has become my touchstone, and I've managed to block out that part of life I'm missing. He picked me up at seven, as promised. He looked wonderful, more formal, more grown-up. I guess I did too. Expensive suits and pretty dresses can do that to people.

"You look great!"

We both said it at the same time. Embarrassing.

"Sorry, I didn't mean to talk over you, but you look beautiful."

"Thank you. And you look very handsome."

"Then we should make a stunning couple, don't you think?"

He offered his arm. I tucked in my hand.

"Well, I know one thing. Margaret would certainly say so!" I could picture her smiling. Made me laugh out loud.

"I guess you need to tell me how Margaret fits into our date."

"Oh she thinks everyone needs 'someone,' and she's convinced herself this dinner will end like a romance novel. That we'll fall madly in love and live happily ever after."

I was still kind of laughing.

He stopped, turned serious, and looked into my eyes.

"And maybe she's right."

Chapter 9

THE MORNING AFTER

Nineteen Years Ago, August

The morning light flooded my room. Nausea was joined by a screaming headache. A raging hangover. Thankfully Sally Ann had already left for class. I needed to move. Greek history was at ten. Keep still. Breathe. It will go away. That's what I told myself. But it didn't. Finally, no choice. I had to get up. I made it to the bathroom and then purged all that lovely wine right out of my body. A relief, but I was still shaky. Quick, cold shower. Dressed. Three Tylenol and then to the cafeteria. I knew I had to eat. Dry toast and hot tea with honey. I slugged through what little breakfast I could eat and went back to my room. I had a few minutes to spare. I took two more Tylenol and then left for class.

I barely made it to the ten o'clock class. It was a lecture day, so no participation required. I had a break until two, so I went back to my room and slept and then walked back to the cafeteria.

I caught up with the group—friends since last year when we were freshmen. We ate together, went to bars together, watched the soaps together, cheered on the 'Horns at football games, helped each other with homework, and told each other our secrets and wishes.

"Well, look who finally showed up," Laura started. I knew it was coming. "We haven't seen you since yesterday afternoon. Where have you been?"

"Yeah," Rita said. "You came back kinda late last night. When you weren't at dinner, we thought it was weird. Then, we were all up late studying in the hallway. We never saw you come in, so it must have been late. We didn't even know you were going out."

"We almost got worried when you didn't show up for breakfast—you never miss a meal." Debbie's turn.

These are my good friends.

Laura from Dallas, short, very athletic, fun.

Debbie from West Texas—Abilene—I think. The oldest,

a senior. Our mother. Nurturing, caring, always ready to give advice—even if you don't ask.

Rita, small-town girl like me. We share that perspective. Beautiful. Always has a boyfriend.

I dreaded seeing them.

"Um, well, you know that class I'm auditing? We had a group session at Schlotz's. Time got away from me."

"And I'm sure a few long-necks for everyone, right?" Laura winked.

"What do you think? Why does anyone really go to Scholtz's?" I laughed and so did they. How easily I lied to my friends.

"Any cute guys in that class? Maybe I'll come next time," Rita joked.

"Not really. There's one guy, Dan, but I think he's got a girlfriend. A pretty nerdy crowd." Don't react.

"So next time just let someone know what's up, so we don't worry. We don't want to get a call from campus police," Debbie warned. "Especially with that Austin rapist still out there!"

A serial rapist had been front page news in Austin for over a month. He had committed five rapes on and around campus. One even happened in a dorm, when a back door was left propped open. We weren't too concerned, but we usually went everywhere in groups of three or more, and the dorms had stepped up security.

"We do have cell phones now," reminded Laura.

"Okay, okay. I'm sorry. It was a last-minute thing after

class. I didn't think it would go long. But I got it. Next time I'll let you know if I'm not going to be around. I really appreciate that you care about me."

And that was it. I was off the hook. No more questions. We ate lunch, joking and laughing, like always. I managed to eat a real meal, well, sort of—PB and J and a Coke. No one asked about a hangover. And after sleeping, I didn't look so bad.

Then we were off, like always.

My two o'clock class was English Lit, one of my favorites. But I couldn't concentrate. Now that I was rested and my stomach settled, I replayed last night over and over. Did I dream it? Seriously, did he kiss me? I was really drunk, so things were hazy. I needed to figure it out.

I went to his classroom as soon as class ended. He was in the middle of teaching, so I sat in the back again. He didn't glance at me when I walked in. Nothing. Maybe I was wrong about last night. It was too late to leave, so I slid back down in my seat and tried to disappear. But I listened.

"God is ever-present—what we will explore is where we find Him hidden in literature. Some places are easy to see—Dante's *Inferno*, for example. Others are more difficult to spot. Any thoughts?"

A petite blond girl in the front row somewhat frantically waved her hand. "Professor, how about *The Lion, the Witch and the Wardrobe* by C.S. Lewis?"

Really, that is so obvious. Are we in junior high?

"Melissa, great example." He smiled at her. Does he really agree?

"Let's talk about that. Who does Aslan represent?"

I tuned the whole thing out. It was ridiculous and stupid and trite. I actually got out other work and started reading. It was too sappy to even watch. I was embarrassed for both of them.

The class lasted another thirty minutes or so. I was ready to bolt as soon as everyone headed out. Obviously, I'd gotten last night all wrong. I was out the door and down the steps when he called to me.

"Vic, wait up."

I should have ignored him and kept going. He sensed my plan, and I walked faster. He caught hold of my arm.

"Wait."

I pulled away. Trying not to be noticeable.

"Why? You're obviously busy," I whispered. I sounded so like an angry girlfriend. I hated it but I felt betrayed somehow.

"No, I'm not. I don't have any more classes today. Do you?"

Is he even kidding me?

"I don't think it matters. You have lots of groupies around." I kept my voice low. I certainly didn't want anyone to hear.

The blond chick stood in the common area just in front of us. Watching. I'm pretty sure she guessed what was going on. I glanced at her. He saw.

"You mean Melissa?" He waved at her. "She's a student in my class. That's it."

"I'm a student in your class."

He paused. "It's not the same. I don't have to give you a grade."

He led me to a picnic table nearby.

"Even if I did have to give you a grade, it wouldn't matter. The truth is you're incredible! I haven't done anything but think about you since last night."

It's all so wrong. I felt jealous and guilty at the same time.

"Oh, really? So that's why you didn't even acknowledge me when I walked in the door?"

"I didn't acknowledge you because it would have totally thrown me off my game. I had to stay engaged and just get through the class. But I felt you the whole time."

Is that really what I wanted to hear?

"Maybe, but then what's with all the 'encouragement' over that ridiculous C.S. Lewis comment? I almost gagged."

"I saw. You tuned out about then. What were you reading?"

"Don't change the subject."

"Do you realize how hard it is to get anyone in a class to participate? Most of them just sit there trying to hide their phones—which is their main focus anyway. I have to work with whatever I get."

He sounded so contrite.

"I understand that, but what's with the goofy eyes at your little friend over there."

She'd followed us and sat down at a different table. Pretending to work on her laptop.

"Vic, I couldn't care less about her. You know professors always have students infatuated with them. She's just one of those. She means nothing. Literally nothing."

I worried she heard him.

"Since I dropped you off last night, all I've thought about is you. I can see you. I can smell you. All I want is to be with you."

His words, the power of his words—was overwhelming. I didn't want to, but I felt the same.

"Look, if you are finished with classes, come somewhere with me. I just bought this house in south Austin. I want to show it to you. Haven't even had time to move in. Maybe you can help me with decorating and that kind of thing."

There was that almost scary feeling from yesterday. It all felt . . . off somehow. But he was so damn handsome, and I really wanted to kiss him again.

"Okay, but I need to tell my friends. They freaked out when I came in so late last night. I can't disappear again. I at least need to call them."

He frowns. Very stern.

"I don't want to bring your friends into this."

"Well, I have to tell them something. I can't just keep disappearing."

"Okay, but you can't tell them about me."

"I thought you weren't worried about what people thought."

He grabs my arm and pulls me close. He whispers, "Do not tell them about me. It will ruin everything."

"Ummm. Please let go. That kind of hurts." He let go. "Okay. I'll tell them I need to study where it's quiet. I go to the main library sometimes."

He smiled. "Great idea."

I smiled back. But I didn't really feel happy.

Chapter 10

LIAR, LIAR, PANTS ON FIRE

Nineteen Years Ago, August

That afternoon he took me to his house. He was right. There was nothing in it except a few towels, toilet paper, and some hand soap. And it was not what I expected. Although, I'm not sure what I did expect. It was a tract home built in an almost ready to be worn-out neighborhood. Two bedrooms, two baths, living room, kitchen, dining nook, and utility room. Attached garage and a very sad and neglected yard. He showed me around, painting verbal pictures of what it would look like after he decorated it. I was dubious. It was going to take a lot of work and money to make that place anything close to special. Not that I was a snob, but I was underwhelmed.

I tried to be complimentary.

"Yes, I can see how color will brighten the room. You're right; all the kitchen needs is a good cleaning. It will be fun to xeriscape the yard."

He knew I wasn't sincere. He finally stopped.

"You hate it, right? I was afraid you would. I should have talked to you before I bought it."

Whoa . . . what did I have to do with it? I didn't even know him when he bought the place.

"Well, to be fair, you didn't know me then. And besides, this is your house. My opinion doesn't count."

He wheeled around. I was walking a step or two behind.

"That is ridiculous. Of course your opinion counts."

Very, very weird.

He pulled me to him. I wanted to resist, but I couldn't. We kissed for a long time.

That was the first time we had sex. I wouldn't call it making love, because it wasn't. It was raw and primal. Greedy. He was slow and skilled. I was an amateur. He made me crazy. It was an experience I'll never forget. Afterward, lying on the carpet, dirty as it was, with his arm around me, I just wanted more.

I made it back to my room by eight-thirty. I told him I

couldn't take a chance on my friends. I was still so nervous and guilty. I needed to get away. It just didn't feel right. I look back now and wonder if I had a premonition of what was to come. After a slow, lingering kiss, he dropped me off about two blocks from the dorm.

From then on, every day was built around ways to be with him. If we had time, we went to the house. I liked that best. And we did get it cleaned, painted, and furnished. Never got around to the yard. In my head, I pretended we were married, and the house was our home. I never said anything like that. I tried to play it cool. But it wasn't a cool situation.

If we couldn't go to the house, I met him in his classroom and we'd sneak to his office and lock the door. It was exhilarating. And still, I felt ashamed. Was I sinning? Did I need forgiveness? But I couldn't resist. I wanted him so much, and he wanted me.

For those few months, I tiptoed around my friends. I doubt they believed my lies. It was a struggle to keep up. I actually wrote some of it down so I could remember. But keeping track of lies is tough, and I tripped up sometimes. Debbie in particular wasn't buying it.

"Victoria, what's up with you? You're never here anymore and even when you are, it seems like you're someplace else."

"Nothing's wrong. You know I'm carrying a heavy load this semester. Eighteen hours and auditing a class. I study all the time and worry about it when I'm not studying."

I was such a fraud. I'd already missed too many classes, and my grades were falling.

"I got that. But there's more to it. Is there a guy?"

"What?" How surprised I acted. "No way. I don't have time for dating. And you know how hard I've worked to get past Bobby. I know it was a high school thing, but still, I'm not going down that road again for a long time."

"I'm just worried. You seem lost to us. You're never around, and when you are here, you're so distracted. What's going on?"

"I'm not. In fact, we're all going to the game this weekend, right? I need a break."

He wasn't happy when I told him I couldn't see him Saturday or Sunday that week. But I didn't have a choice. He was a professor, and I was a student. I needed and wanted to spend time with my friends. I just hoped he would change his mind about them after the semester ended.

The weekend passed too quickly. I relaxed, laughed, and drank beer. We went to the game and stood and yelled with the rest of our 20,000 closest friends. I didn't realize how much I'd missed everyone. I didn't realize how different life was without lies and the knot in the pit of my stomach. I almost told them about him. But I couldn't—whether from shame or fear, I'm not sure.

After that one "normal" weekend, I limped along, juggling my friends, school, time with him, and my family. I lied to them too. I missed a few trips home, and I let many of their calls go to voicemail. Mom and Dad said they missed me and wished I could come home for a visit. But they didn't ask many questions. Thank God. Like God would have anything to do with me. I lied to Him too.

Even my professors were worried. Several called me in for a conference. My 3.8 GPA dropped to 2.4. I blamed everything on my heavy load. It made some sense, so I skated by, skimming the surface of truth.

We'd been seeing each other about a month when I first noticed a change in his behavior. It was subtle, but he was less gentle, less kind, less giving. I thought I was imagining it. I tried to believe that—until I couldn't.

We'd managed to get a whole day and night together. I don't remember how. It was a Saturday. We took our time, saw a movie, ate, and then went to the house. We didn't talk much. It was nice to just be together—at least for me it was. Several times he mentioned other guys.

"So, do you ever wish I was younger?"

"No, silly. I love you."

"Do you want something I'm not giving you?"

I grinned. "We could talk about God, since, well, since that was the original reason we met."

"You think I tricked you? Used God as a seduction?"

"No, of course not. I think we found other things to process."

I smiled again. He didn't.

"You know other men watch you." No segue to this topic.

"What do you mean watch me? Women watch you too."

"Not the same. I'm not interested in them."

"And you think I'm interested in other men? That's ridiculous."

He grabbed my arm—hard. "Ow, stop. That hurts." I remembered saying something like that before—in fact, the whole thing was a little déjà vu.

His grip tightened.

"You think I don't know, but I do."

"Please stop. That really hurts, and I have no idea what you're talking about."

He slapped me. My head rocked back.

"What are you doing?"

It hurt like hell, and I was still in his unyielding grip.

After that, I quit talking and just defended myself against the blows. Crying, sobbing. He was relentless. I couldn't shake him or stop him. And then he raped me. I didn't say no. I was too scared, but I wanted to. This wasn't about love—it was power, dominion, control.

He apologized after. Said he didn't know what happened. Said he loved me so much he couldn't stand the idea of any other man even looking me. Begged my forgiveness. Said it would never happen again. But, of course, it did. More and more often.

Chapter 11

KEY TO MY HEART

We'd been inseparable after that Friday. We actually stopped working every weekend. Shocking, I know. Starting each Friday, we played. We went to movies. Hiked the Berkshire Trails—not all, but some. Ate nice dinners. And watched baseball games—live if the Sox played at home.

The Saturday after the first dinner, we'd gone to see a movie, *No Country for Old Men*. I'd read the book and really wanted to see it. Liam agreed—wanting to make me happy back then.

"Not sure I liked it," he said as we were leaving the theater.

"Cormac McCarthy's books are always dark, but they haunt you. You can't always have a happy ending."

"But that's what I want—happy endings. Could we have that?"

Seemed a bit too soon to talk about endings for me.

"A happy ending? Maybe so. Too early to tell, don't you think?"

"I don't know. I think we could. How 'bout having dinner at my place?" At this point, I'd never been there. I wasn't sure I was ready. Too many old memories.

"What would we eat? Do you even keep food in the house?" I joked.

"You'd be surprised. I'm a great cook. I thought maybe you'd agree to dinner, so I've got things ready—if you want to go."

He was so cute. I could see the little boy in him, waiting to see if I'd come out to play. But it was presumptuous how he already bought meal preparations. In the end, I took the chance.

He lived alone, like me, in a townhouse too, not as big as mine, but nice. Decorated with a man's touch—more leather, more dark colors, a bigger TV. It felt homey and comfortable. And, he was, in fact, a very good cook. Chicken marsala, tender and perfectly seasoned, a fresh salad, and what looked like homemade bread. We shared a bottle of Chianti and talked about our families and our past—at least the part I was willing to share. Crème brûlée for dessert—the real deal with a kitchen torch and all. I was a bit more than impressed.

As the days went by, I became more and more comfortable with Liam. He was funny, kind, and ready for any adventure. We spent a lot of time making out, but I wasn't ready for anything more. Until one Sunday afternoon after we'd been seeing each other about three months. We were at his place. We were trying to decide where to eat dinner.

"We could stay here. I've got enough around to throw together a meal." He came up behind me as I was looking out the window. I felt his breath on my neck. Looking back, it was his genuine kindness and patience that helped me along. I turned to him.

"Yes, I think we should stay here. But maybe dinner could wait a bit."

He knew what I meant. I can't say I wasn't nervous, but he knew what he was doing and was slow and careful. He knew I'd been badly hurt in the past—not how, exactly, but he knew I was scared. Slowly and carefully, he pushed all the right buttons. Found magic places. He was gentle and tender. He held me and talked to me and paid attention to me. We fit together. For the first time in a very long time, I felt safe.

I think I was happy. It's really hard to remember. But it seems like I was. Happiness had eluded me for so long, I had no baseline to judge. Liam made me smile. He so wanted to please me. You'd think he'd won some kind of grand prize. He said things like, "I can't believe you want me!" or, "I knew I loved you the first time I saw you," and "I just want to spend the rest of my life with you." It sounded so nice, but even then, in the early days, I heard an echo of another voice. A voice that demanded control. I dismissed it immediately. I wanted to be happy—and so I believed I was.

And, he adored me. Adoration is seductive. I remembered that seduction but convinced myself it was totally different this time. I knew he loved me more than I loved him, but being on a pedestal is a heady experience. It's hard to come down to reality. So, I let things go on.

If Liam stayed at my house, Jim drove us both to work. Julie cooked for us, and if either of them disapproved, they never said anything to me. And he stayed at my place more and more often.

For her part, Margaret was, as they say, over the moon. She kept saying things like, "I just knew this would happen," or "you two were meant for each other," or "you make such a cute couple." I told her to settle down.

Liam constantly pressed about the future, but I didn't want to think about it. I just lived it one day at a time. Sometimes he would get angry when I didn't play along.

"Why won't you talk about plans with me?" I heard that several times and always in a scornful, demanding voice.

I did my best to soothe things over. Sometimes I would even speculate with him about where we might live next. But I was also worried about our jobs. We decided to talk to upper management about us. Didn't want them to hear from someone else. In the end, it was no problem. They knew we would both get our work done. They wanted to keep their racehorses happy. What's it all about anyway? The money.

And we made money for them. Worry crossed off the list. The worry about the future didn't go away as easily.

Liam was far more social than me. To be honest, who wasn't? As a true extrovert, he forced me out into the light. We went to lots of parties, met friends for drinks or dinner or brunch. We threw our own parties. People came too. Between my fabulous house, Julie's fantastic food, and Liam's charisma, no one missed a Nelson-Campbell production.

Honestly, the parties were fun—until they weren't. The more often we had people over, and especially if I suggested it, the more resentful and jealous Liam became. Several times he quizzed me.

"Who were you talking to in the hall today?"

"Why did you spend so much time with Mike at the party?"

"Did you see those guys watching you when we walked in? I don't want you to talk to them!"

In general, I played it down. Gave explanations, told him he was wrong, and most of the time, it worked. Or, at least it seemed to.

Overall, it exhausted me. I have no idea how we kept up with work, but we did. We were rising stars. I waited for the crash, but it didn't come. Not until right before Thanksgiving.

We'd been dating for over six months. We were at my house. I was reading for work, and Liam was on the computer.

"So, Vic, I've checked the airlines. I think we need to book the flight to Texas before the best seats are taken."

When did we talk about going to Texas together?

"Ummm, I haven't given it much thought. Sometimes I book at the last minute. You'd be surprised at the deals you can get if you wait."

"You don't need deals, what do you mean? Do you want to fly United or American—we have first-class either way."

Panic. I'm not ready for this—Liam and my family.

"Do you really want to meet my family? I didn't think you were up for that. And what about your family? Don't you want to see them?"

"Yes, I want to meet your family, silly. I know how important they are to you. I need to meet them myself. Besides, they should meet your boyfriend. And, my family is fine. I told them we'd go there for Christmas."

I'm sweating, and it's twenty-four degrees with a smattering of snow on the ground. Did we talk about this and I forgot? No. Not possible. And, I'd never agreed to go to Seattle for Christmas! I'm sure of that. I could barely breathe. Liam didn't notice.

"So, I think the United flight is our best bet. One short layover in Baltimore."

"I usually fly Southwest," I quickly responded. "They have a direct flight into Austin, and they're dependable."

"Southwest, are you kidding me?" Liam liked his money— and mine, and, if given the chance, he preferred to use mine. "They don't even have reserved seats. It's a four-hour flight. We need to be in first-class."

"No, we don't. And it's not that bad. We can go business

class. They board first. I like the direct flight. Don't be such a snob."

What am I doing? I should stop this. I shouldn't encourage him. But I don't want him to be disappointed or, worse yet, angry. When he was angry, it took so long for him to get over it. He pouted like a petulant child.

"Fine. There's a morning flight." He was definitely sulking.

"How early?"

This is crazy. Why don't I say something? Why don't I stop this?

"Seven fifty-five."

"That's fine. I'll be up anyway."

"Okay—your credit card or mine?" He could easily afford the trip. It would have been nice if he just paid.

"I don't care." I inwardly sighed. "We could meet that new prospect in Austin before we come back and write it off to the company."

Look at me, planning this trip, even getting reimbursement.

"Great idea! That's one of the reasons I love you. Always thinking. I'll use the company card. Working on it now." It was amazing how he could rebound from that mad kid when he got his way.

I watched him, slouched on the couch, fingers flying across the keyboard. Looks like it will be Thanksgiving in Texas.

Chapter 12

GOING HOME

Traveling from Boston to Texas is easy. It's a four hour direct flight. We landed about noon, Texas time. We'd been up since five-thirty, Boston time. Jim dropped us at Boston Logan International Airport at six forty-five. We checked bags, trudged through security, and were at the gate with thirty minutes to spare. It was too close for my comfort. I like to be at the gate no later than an hour and a half before boarding. Liam didn't think we needed that much time for such an early flight. It wasn't worth the fight.

Boarding started fifteen minutes after we arrived.

It was one-thirty before we drove out of the Hertz lot in Austin. We were both hungry and grumpy.

"You need to eat." Liam was driving. It makes me so angry when he says that, even if it is true.

"We both do. You're as grouchy as I am."

"I'm not grouchy. Just tired." Because you didn't go to sleep until midnight, I think.

"Whatever. You'd better take off that sweater and kick up the AC too, or you're going to stroke out."

"Will you just give me a minute! I'm trying to find the way out." He was tired and frustrated. I should have insisted on driving.

"If you would have let me drive, we'd be out."

"Stop it! Just stop it. I've had enough of you already today. Just quit talking." He practically shouted at me.

Off to a great start. I did what he asked. I quit talking. I knew this routine.

No Lake LBJ this year. Mom and Dad said it was time to come home. So, after grabbing food to go at Whataburger, we spent a quiet two hours driving to the ranch. Hated to admit it, but I was hungry. Noncommittal, Liam ate his burger. I didn't ask how he liked it. Practically the state burger, but . . . oh well. I quit talking.

I had called my parents the week before and asked if I could bring Liam with me. Mom said of course. Dad didn't say anything. To be fair, I hadn't talked to them much about Liam. I wasn't sure what to say or what to call our relationship. Of course, I talked about this and mentioned things we were doing, but I didn't give them much indication of the seriousness of our relationship.

On one of his biannual visits in September, William met us for dinner. He was in Boston for a legal conference, as it turned out. It was a pleasant evening with the guys talking sports. I interjected from time to time, but mostly I watched them. I wanted to see if William approved. In his typical charming way, with William, I couldn't tell either way. He is always gracious. And, I didn't ask. Maybe I didn't want to know.

So, between conversations with Mom and Dad and William's visit, I thought my family was prepared for our arrival. As it turns out, I couldn't have been more wrong.

Besides Mom and Dad, Liam and I were the only ones staying at the house. I wondered what Mom would want us to do. Separate rooms? Same room? It didn't matter to me.

About a half-hour out, it was time to talk.

"Look, you can be mad if you want, but we'd better figure out a few things before we get to my parents."

Side glance. Both hands on the wheel. No response.

"I'm sure Mom doesn't know what to do about sleeping arrangements. I want my parents to feel comfortable, so I think we should stay in separate rooms."

That got his attention.

"That's ridiculous! We're adults for God's sake. No one expects that."

"Maybe not, but it'll still be less awkward for them."

"For them or for you? Did you even want me to come on this trip?"

I hate when he's angry. But I'd been less than enthusiastic about the trip. He knew it. I was trying, but, still, he knew.

"Honestly, Liam, it's not a big deal. It's three days. And, of course I wanted you to come. Why are you being like this?"

"Like what? Oh, pissed off? Well, let's see. You've barely talked to me since I bought the tickets. You tried to back out twice, and now you tell me we have to act like kids. Maybe that's it. Ya think?"

Really, really angry. This was bad. My chest was tight. I started to panic. We were too close to home for drama. I reached into my purse and grabbed my bottle.

"Listen to me. Stop the car. Just pull over."

"What? We'll get killed."

"People do it all the time out here. But if you want, pull into that Exxon station ahead."

He did and left the car running.

"Please look at me."

He turned to face me. Mad but hurt too. Just like him when things don't go his way.

"This part of Texas is very, very different from Boston. I know you've spent time in Austin, but it's very, very different from Austin too. People live a much simpler life. Things tend to be more black and white here. It's . . . it's kind of old fashioned."

He looked down. Was he hearing me? Oftentimes, I wondered.

"I don't want us to make a bad impression with my family. I want them to like you, and they will. But we need to remember it's better to play by their rules or ideas or whatever you want to call it."

He glanced at me. Seemed he might be better or maybe the pill was working. Either way.

"So, could we just be happy? Try to enjoy ourselves and not make a big deal about things like separate rooms?"

"I'm sorry."

He had that hangdog look—almost as bad as being angry.

"I'm just so keyed up. I really do want your family, especially your parents, to approve of me. I'm just super nervous."

"I know. Me too. Trust me on this. Just follow my lead. It'll be fine."

He leans forward and gives me a kiss. Crisis over. I feel myself relax just a bit. Maybe it will be alright after all.

"Okay, okay." Smiling. "We can do this, right?"

"Right."

Thinking back now, it was stupid to try. Liam was right. I didn't want him to come. Being back home was rough for me in the best of circumstances—and the trip with Liam didn't feel like the best of circumstances. The last two months had been difficult at best. Between the sulking, the jealousy, and the general controlling attitude, I was about done. I genuinely liked Liam. He was a nice guy, but the moodiness, the distraction, the possessiveness—it was wearing on me.

I just had to get through the trip.

We made it to the house close to five o'clock. As we drove

down the road to the house, I opened my window. Mom and Dad own almost 1,500 acres. Some of it is irrigated cropland, but most of it is pasture. Dad and the ranch hands run about six hundred head of cattle, mostly Brangus. The pastures provide good grass for the cattle and lots of cover and vegetation for other wildlife. Dad also stocks about eighty goats. As a kid growing up, I loved the baby goats. We'd climb into the pens and run around with them—until we got caught. Dad said the animals, especially the mommas, needed to be calm and we shouldn't upset them. He asked me one time how I thought Mom would feel if someone was chasing me all around the yard, scaring me. I had always thought I was playing with the babies, but maybe not.

There are three sets of cattle pens on the ranch and one for the goats. Windmills and cattle troughs are scattered everywhere for the livestock and the wildlife.

Hunting is a big thing in our county. October is the start of deer season. Lots of unfamiliar faces in town during hunting season. The locals complain sometimes, but hunting brings good money to not only the county but the town, too. So, no one complains that much.

Dad doesn't lease the ranch for hunting. He's been asked many times over the years, but he keeps it to friends and family only. When we were kids, hunting was part of Thanksgiving. Dad made schedules so that everyone who wanted to hunt had a chance—friends, cousins, uncles, even some aunts. The family hunted anytime, so it was Dad's way to give back.

In mid-November, you could usually see the beginning of the winter gloom in the plants and trees, even if it was still hot. This year, though, there'd been a lot of rain. It kept everything alive and green longer than usual. The place looked great.

Mom and Dad came out to greet us when the car stopped. They looked older but somehow the same. Mom waved and walked down the front steps. We met in front of the car and hugged. I almost cried. Dad was right behind her. He hugged me too and kissed my cheek. There was that dad smell—sweat and Old Spice. I almost cried again.

Dad reached out to shake Liam's hand, "David Campbell."

Liam shook his hand. "Liam. Liam Nelson. It's very nice to finally meet you, and you too, Mrs. Campbell."

"Pooh, call me Carolyn. And call him David. No need for formality here."

"Okay, well, then. Good to meet you both, David and Carolyn."

"Let's go inside out of this heat. I'll bet you guys are thirsty and maybe hungry. Did you get a chance to eat?"

Mom started back up the steps. The big, wood frame house sits on a small knoll about two miles from the public road. My grandparents built it in 1938. Mom and Dad added on after they moved in, and it's been remodeled several times over the years. Mom likes to re-do.

A long front porch complete with rocking chairs and

swings winds around the house. We've spent a lot of time out on the porch. It's well-loved.

The master bedroom, bath, kitchen, and main living room are on the first floor, and four bedrooms and three baths are upstairs. There's another living area upstairs that was "the kids' room." We all spent many hours there, playing pool or watching TV with friends.

Mom wanted a swimming pool, so before I was born, Dad had one built behind the house. Mom said she wanted the pool so everyone would come to our house. She got her wish. In the summer, we'd have pool parties almost every week.

There are three other houses on the ranch. A guest house, the bunkhouse, and the North House. The guest house and bunkhouse are used often. The North House was Mom and Dad's first home. By the time I was born, they were living in the big house. It is only used on rare occasions when large groups come to stay.

"I'll help with your bags." Dad walked to the trunk.

"That's not necessary. I can get them."

"No, I'll help." Not a request, a statement. Dad is like that.

Dad and Liam brought in our luggage and left it at the bottom of the stairs. Mom and I were in the kitchen.

"Come in here, you two. I've got iced tea and some sand-wiches. Something to tide us over until supper. Everyone else should be here about seven. David is going to barbecue. Turkey tomorrow."

Finally, I could really eat. I don't know how, but Mom always makes the best sandwiches. I've made sandwiches with the very same ingredients but it's never like Mom's. And sweet tea—I forgot how much I like it.

We talked for a while, small talk—how was the trip? What's the weather like in Boston? It's been dry here. Gus is playing t-ball. Nothing major. Just getting to know you stuff. Mom and I did the majority of talking but Liam joined in, and like always, he pretty much took over from there. Dad mostly listened.

"So, Liam. How much has Victoria told you about our family?" Liam glanced at me, questioning.

"Mom, seriously, I've told him about everyone. But if you want, you are welcome to do your own spin."

It came out harsher than I intended.

"I'm sorry, Mom. I mean. I think it would be good for you to tell Liam. I've been gone for so long, and I'm probably not up to speed."

Mom's usually a good sport.

"Well, let me see. Our oldest child is William. He and his wife, Susie, met in law school at UT. You do know about UT, don't you?"

"How could I not? We have to watch every game Texas plays—in any sport."

"Good. That's the way it should be. William practices criminal law in San Antonio, but they live here in town. They have the two boys, Gus and Franklin. I'm sure Victoria talks about them. Don't tell Annie, but she's their favorite. She spoils them rotten!"

I rolled my eyes.

"Yes, of all the family, other than you and David, she talks about the boys the most. I can't wait to meet them. They sound like terrific little guys."

"Of course, I'm biased, but they are so wonderful. And funny—they say such silly things. Susie quit practicing law after Gus was born—he's five. He started kindergarten this year, and he thinks he is very grown-up. He acts like it too. Franklin is three. And smart. They are so smart. And they love dinosaurs. Gus knows the names of all of them—from T. rex to stegosaurus."

Mom is proud of all of us; the grandkids are special, though.

"When I was a kid, I loved dinosaurs too," Liam said. "My dad took me to lots of exhibits so I could see 'real' dinosaurs."

"Most boys like them. Both our boys did, too."

"I guess that's true. Go on, Carolyn."

"Annie is next in line. She teaches sixth-grade math at the middle school. She's on maternity leave right now. She just had our granddaughter, Chloe, eight months ago. And she is so precious. She's crawling everywhere now, Vicky."

"I can't wait to see her. Where is she going to stay when Annie goes back to work?"

"Annie found a wonderful woman to come and stay at

the house until Chloe is older. Hopefully that will work out." Mom didn't seem worried.

"I think I said Annie's husband is Derek. Derek played football at Texas Tech and he's the head coach and athletic director here. We had a winning season. Made it to semifinals. Got beat there. We were all disappointed."

"Poor ole Bobcats. But that's still good for Derek, right?"

"Right. Course everyone wants to win state, but we still did well. Let me see. Next is Christopher. He's president of Texas Central Bank in San Antonio. His wife, Jennifer, is a nurse. She works at Northeast Baptist Hospital. They were high school sweethearts. They live in San Antonio."

"Are they coming tonight?"

"No, they both had to work today. I think Jennifer has the late shift, so they won't be here until tomorrow."

"I miss goofy ole Chris. I haven't seen him since Easter. Did he lose that weight he's always talking about?"

"Not really, but don't say anything about it. He's still trying."

Mom, Dad, and I smile. It's a running joke with Christopher that he needs to lose weight. He really doesn't. He might be a few pounds heavier than college, but that's all. He still thinks he's the stud he was in high school. Quarterback of the football team. Basketball and baseball too.

"Then, Victoria, our baby." Mom smiled at me, but, thankfully, the family history was over.

"I just noticed it's already six-thirty. We'd better get

things going before the rest of the family gets here. David, why don't you and Liam get the barbecue pit ready?"

"I've got it. I don't need help." Dad headed out the back door.

"I guess I'll just take our things upstairs, then." Liam sounded off. Probably felt left out. Not the greatest start.

"Good idea. Victoria, you know where things are. Go get settled in."

"Okay, but which two rooms do you want us to use?"

Mom started on a green salad but didn't flinch when I asked.

"Why don't you use Chris and Annie's rooms? They each have their own baths. I made them up this morning."

I'd been right on the separate bedroom call. I looked at Liam and mouthed, "See what I mean?" No response.

Annie and Derek came in about twenty minutes later. Annie carried potato salad and a basket of homemade rolls. She's almost as good as Mom in the kitchen. Derek carried Chloe.

After hugs and kisses, I introduced them to Liam. They were polite, but we all got caught up playing with Chloe.

"I'm an only child, so I don't have much experience with babies or even little kids," Liam tried to join in.

Maybe it was the way he said it, as though he might not want kids. Whatever it was, Mom and Derek both caught it and paused a second. Derek raised an eyebrow. I just shrugged and turned back to talk about the baby.

"At this point, Chloe may be one too. She's still not sleeping through the night."

Annie and Derek are usually almost telepathic. I was surprised she didn't pick up on the nuance in Liam's statement, but she was sleep-deprived, so who knows.

The awkward moment passed, but it wasn't the last one. Before dinner, I took another pill. It had been four hours, so it was fine. By the time everyone left, I just wanted to sleep. Mom, Dad, and I cleaned up. Liam offered to help, but he was a guest, and guests don't help, although I think he should have. It would have scored points with all of us. Dad made him a drink and told him we'd meet him on the porch.

We worked pretty much in silence. I finished drying the last bowl.

"If you don't care, I'm going to head to bed. I'm so tired, I can't keep moving." I cared about Mom and Dad, but at that point, I didn't care what Liam thought. I was tired and had been on edge for too long.

"Of course, sweetie. Go to bed. We'll tell Liam."

"Thanks, Dad."

I barely made it upstairs. I managed to wash my face and brush my teeth, but that was it. After that, I crashed.

Chapter 13

TURKEY DAY

No one made it to the house before noon, which was a good thing. Mom and I hustled to get the mashed potatoes and green bean casserole ready. She'd been up since six when she started the turkey. I wasn't far behind. I got the dressing ready. It would go into the roaster about an hour before we ate. Getting the Thanksgiving meal ready is an exercise in timing, preparation, and coordination. Mom was an expert. We'd done it so many times, I knew the moves, too. We worked in parallel patterns, managing the dishes as we went.

"Liam seems very nice. How long have you two been dating?"

I helped myself to a cup of coffee and sat down at the kitchen table, the little one we used every day.

"Oh, um, he is nice. We've been together about six months."

"Well, what else? Have you met his parents?"

"No, and like he said, he's an only child, so he wants us to go there for Christmas."

To Mom's credit, she didn't overreact. "Well, I can understand that. But I hope there will be some way that you can come home, too."

Maybe because it was early or maybe because it was just the two of us, but whatever, I started talking.

"You know, Mom. I'm not sure I'll go to Seattle. Actually, I'm not sure we will be together at Christmas."

She didn't interrupt.

"I mean, I do like Liam. He's very nice. But I don't think I'm in love with him. I really didn't even want him to come with me this weekend. It just kind of happened."

I started crying. Mom came to me and pulled me into a tight hug.

"Honey, it's okay. These things tend to work out how they should."

"I know, but I just can't ever seem to get it right. Know what I mean? What's wrong with me?"

"Victoria Jean, stop that. You are one of the strongest, most accomplished women I know. Look at all you've been through; how successful you are. You don't have anything wrong."

She pulled away to see if I was paying attention.

"Now listen to me. No matter what, you do not settle for second-best. If Liam isn't the one, then he just isn't. We'll be nice to him and get through this weekend together, but then, go home and end it, if this is how you really feel. There's no use hanging onto something that won't work and is already over."

We just rocked together.

"Sweetheart, no one is normal—and everyone is normal. We're all just human beings doing our best in the world. Everything is okay. Just have some faith."

Mom has great, unshakable faith. Sometimes I do, but not always.

About eight-thirty, Liam came into the kitchen. Mom gave him a cup of coffee and visited with him. He stayed in the kitchen with Mom and me, doing most of the talking. I tuned him out. I wondered how I would make the entire three days. I kept asking myself if I could just avoid him. Then I felt guilty for thinking that.

William, Susie, and the boys were first to arrive. I heard them before I saw them. The boys came screaming into the kitchen.

"Aunt Vicky! Aunt Vicky! You're here!"

Nothing melts me like those two little men. They threw their arms around my legs, almost pulling me over. My heart sang.

"Hey guys, careful. I don't want to fall and hurt you."

"You won't! Got presents for us?"

"Boys! Really, is that the way you should act?"

Susie walked in with a chocolate pie; William followed with pecan and coconut cream. Susie is a fabulous baker. It doesn't matter what the occasion is, we can always count on her to bring delicious and often decadent desserts. Thanksgiving tradition dictated she bring pies.

"It's okay, Susie."

I leaned down and giggled with the boys.

"Those pies look amazing."

"Thanks. I was worried I wouldn't get them done in time."

Susie gave me a kiss on the check, set down her pie, and reached for the ones William was carrying.

"Hey, little sis! How are you? We've missed you." William pulled me into a big ole bear hug, lifting me off the ground.

"I'm good. I'm good. I've missed you guys too."

Liam cleared his throat.

"Um, guys? Liam, you know William. This is his wife, Susie. And these two little monsters are Gus and Franklin."

The boys hid behind my legs.

"Good to see you again, William. Nice to meet you Susie. Hey guys, how about a high five?" Liam put up his right hand for a slap.

The boys shrank back.

"Boys, give Liam a high five," William encouraged.

But they wouldn't. Dogs and children know the truth

about people. No matter what Liam tried that weekend, they never did give him a high five.

"They're just shy," Susie said.

Mom put the salad we'd made earlier on the sideboard.

"They just need to get to know you, Liam. Don't worry about it." William tickled Franklin.

"Oh, I remember being their ages. It's fine."

But he was offended. I could tell. It wasn't so much what he said, but how he said it. Clip. Short. I don't know what he expected—these were children after all.

Chapter 14

MAD, MAD WORLD

Nineteen Years Ago, November

This time of year was my favorite: the end of football season and Christmas coming. Campus was so beautiful. The searing summer sun reluctantly retreating into the background of life. We call it autumn, but it's not a real autumn. Not like in Boston.

In Boston, around August, the trees begin to shed the bounty of leaves that multiplied during the spring and summer. Temperatures drop and sweaters and sweatshirts come out of storage. Of course, native Bostonians don't get out sweaters or, God forbid, coats until the end of September. Years of living in subzero cold and almost continuous snow for three to four months of the year harden them. I never reached that point. I kept layers ready almost year-round.

But in Texas, late October to even December, it's usually still warm. Up to seventy or eighty degrees isn't unusual. Overall, it just feels better. You can breathe—actually walk outside and move around without thinking you might pass out. The leaves don't change color like they do in the East; most transform into leafless skeletons and stay that way until the following spring. It's sad in a way, but hopeful too. You always know the leaves will come back. The relentless, rainless days pass as well. When hurricane season starts in the Gulf, we generally catch some of the inland deposit. Some years, it causes flooding. Always the extreme in Texas—bone dry or flooding.

I struggled daily during that autumn. Getting out of bed took a superhuman amount of energy. I went to class in a daze, and it amazes me now that I maintained even that 2.4 GPA. I don't remember doing any reading, outside work, or even taking tests. I guess I did. I must have.

Have you ever had a time in your life where you looked like you were functioning like everyone else? You smiled; you carried on conversations with lots of people; you were even in pictures. But you don't remember any of it. My theory is the front part of the brain made you function, somewhat like normal, but the back part of your brain—the part that remembers and absorbs the day to day—that part was totally and absolutely preoccupied with something else. When that "something else" is over, you look at those pictures, and nothing about them is familiar. It's self-preservation, a kind of survival. My therapist agrees.

That was me back then. I must have seemed normal— at least for a while. As the constant worry, continual lying, mainstay of guilt, and overwhelming fear took over, maybe I wasn't. Life was a struggle. I stopped eating and lost about twenty pounds. On a small frame like mine, I looked very sick. My friends thought I had an eating disorder and later they told me they wondered and worried constantly what was wrong with me.

I didn't go out anymore, either. I stuck to the story of the ridiculously packed class schedule, that it was killing me that I needed to "study" all the time. I kept going to the main library. I told everyone it was easier to concentrate there. Another lie.

All that time, he wove a hypnotic spell, pulling me deeper into his lair of control. I was panicked and afraid. The pattern of seeing each other continued, but more and more he only wanted to go to the house. He was paranoid someone would find out about us. I couldn't go to his office or meet him in his classroom anymore. He made me drop his class since I was just auditing anyway. I didn't have the energy to protest. We rarely ate out, and if we did, it was at a place far, far from campus.

Sometimes I wondered who people thought we were when we walked into a restaurant. I doubt we looked like a couple. I was nineteen and he was thirty-nine, turning forty that October. I looked like a kid, and he was a grown man. It's embarrassing now to think about it. My therapist says I shouldn't dwell on it, and most days I don't. I try to stay present.

It became our routine for him to pick me up, usually in the evening, on the darkest corner of Red River. It meant I had to walk about a mile, but by that time, I didn't have the strength to object. Then he would drive to the house. At one point, he noticed a neighbor watering plants outside when we pulled up. It was still early evening, still a bit of light out. After that, he made me hide on the floorboard from the time we drove into the subdivision until the garage door closed. We never spent any time outside.

I still thought I loved him. I needed to believe that. How else could I justify what was happening to me? But, I couldn't understand how he changed or why. And as hard as I tried to be good, he always said I wasn't.

He criticized my clothes—too sexy or not sexy enough. He criticized my lack of education, said I was stupid. He criticized my cooking. Nothing I did seemed to make him happy. And oh, how I tried. I cleaned the house, did his laundry, made him drinks, and played along with all his weird sexual fantasies. To this day, I can't talk about most of that, even with my therapist. I remember two things clearly—the pain and the humiliation. I guess that was the point.

But no matter what I did, almost every time, I was punished. If I wasn't too bad, it was a slap or maybe a push against the wall. On the worst days, it was a beating. Fists, kicks, pulling me by the hair, bruising holds—but you gotta give it to him, he was strategic. Clothes and long sleeves covered his work. The few times I got bruises on my face, I used concealer and wore sunglasses until the green-purple bruising passed. Who knew what my friends thought?

I longed for the earlier days, and just often enough, the man I first knew came back. On those rare occasions, he was kind and gentle and all about me. That's probably the reason I kept going back. For those days. And because I was afraid. He'd done a good job. I did think I was bad, a failure, incredibly stupid. For so long, it was only his opinion I heard in my head. And that's what I came to believe.

How long did this last? Maybe three months? I'm not sure. Each morning, I felt the pressure building the moment I woke up. When I stumbled home at the end of the day, I couldn't let it go. I knew it would start again the next day.

My friends kept at me.

"Nothing is wrong. Why are you guys so keyed up? I'm just about to lose it with this studying. I didn't realize how hard this was going to be. I wish I hadn't started this schedule, but I have to stick it out. Just get through it."

"We get that," Deb frowned, "but you need to start eating. You've lost so much weight. You don't look good, and you're going to get sick."

"Well, thanks a lot. I might have lost a little weight, but I'm eating plenty."

"You are not. We watch you. You just pick at your food.

And you're always somewhere else. Half the time you don't even hear what we're saying."

I couldn't take their kindness, and I couldn't tell them anything.

"Just worry about yourselves, how 'bout that, and leave me alone." I had to be angry so they would stop. "I'm doing fine! I really don't need the extra pressure from you guys right now. Okay?"

I'd stomp out of the room. And then go take a shower and sob uncontrollable, hiccuping sobs under the hottest water I could stand. I knew they knew I was lying. I just hoped they'd leave me alone.

I found out later that Deb called my parents and told them how worried they were. Mom was immediately upset, but Dad was calmer. He thought my class schedule could be the problem. They all agreed my parents would talk to me when I went home for Thanksgiving.

Except I didn't go home. I came up with another excuse—a major exam the week after Thanksgiving. I had to stay and study. Mom and Dad didn't like it. They almost came and got me, but I promised I'd come home the weekend after my test. I sometimes wonder what would have happened if they had come. Doesn't matter now.

So, I stayed while everyone else went home. There were a few RAs left in the dorm, a few girls from out of state, but overall, the place was pretty much deserted.

In a way, it was a relief. I didn't have to pretend or lie. And I was with him most of the time, anyway. I called my parents on Thanksgiving Day, with him watching me, waiting for me to screw up. Just hearing the sounds of my family back home made me so very sad and homesick. I almost cried, but I didn't. I knew I couldn't.

After the call, he said, "You know from now on, I'm all the family you need."

It wasn't a question; it was an order. I didn't respond.

"Well, don't you agree? I'm not even sure you need to finish college. We could move. Go to Colorado or somewhere and start over. No one would know us. What about that?"

What about that? The thought was terrifying, but I said, "I think that would be great, but I would really like to finish college. At the end of this semester, I'll only have two more years."

"Well that's not going to happen. At least not here in Austin. I'm not waiting around much longer. We should leave right after the semester ends."

And that was that. No more conversation and certainly no discussion.

One time during that holiday, I reminded him of our first conversation, about how he was going to help me process my relationship with God. He mocked me.

"Do you really think God wants anything to do with you? You're lucky you have me. I have a personal relationship with God. You have a long way to go. You need to be a better person. You know the Bible says the man is the head of the household. You need to learn that—completely. You need to respect my decisions and do as I say. Then maybe someday, you'll be ready to know God."

He was wrong. I knew that. God loved me, but I was so totally messed up by that point, I couldn't feel God anywhere in my world.

Several days before classes ended for the holiday, I'd seen him on campus with Melissa—remember her? He had his arm around her, their heads close together, talking and laughing. I made it to the nearest bathroom and vomited. What was going on? He had said she meant nothing. I wanted to ask him about it then, but I didn't have the courage. But then, on Thanksgiving Day at his house, I thought of it again.

"Hey, guess what? I saw you walking campus with one of your students a couple of days ago."

He stopped what he was doing, reading, I think. He went still. I should have stopped then. I knew the signs. But I wanted to know.

"You were with Melissa, the girl from your class. You know, the C.S. Lewis chick. Are you tutoring her?"

He didn't speak. He just sat, very calm and looked at me for several minutes. I almost squirmed, but I didn't.

"It is NONE of your business what I do in my professional life or with my students. You are NOT to spy or eavesdrop on me EVER again."

I should have acquiesced.

"I wasn't spying or eavesdropping. I just happened to see you near Seton Hall. I was on my way to class."

He rose from the chair and walked to me. I couldn't move. I saw that look in his eyes, and I knew I'd gone too far. I tried to backtrack.

"I'm sorry I brought it up. I know you care about your students. It's one of the things I love about you."

It was too late.

He stood in front of me, grabbed both my arms, and threw me across the room, hard. I slid down the living room wall and landed on my butt. He kept coming. I rolled on my side and covered my head with my arms. He kicked my legs and my stomach. I think he might have cracked a few ribs. He picked me up by my hair and pulled me to the bedroom. He pulled down my pants, ripped off my panties—everything was pain. He slapped me twice, once on each side of my face. Then, he just looked at me. He shook his head and took off his jeans. And then he plunged into me. I felt like my body was being torn in two. But I didn't make a sound. It was fast and over.

"There is no one else, remember that. I will NEVER let you leave me. Do you understand?"

"Yes, I understand."

He kissed me tenderly. I wanted to cringe, but I had to respond.

"And you know I hate to punish you. You need to stop upsetting me. It's your fault, you know."

"Yes, I know."

"Okay then, how about we make that stir-fry together?"

No traditional holiday meal that day.

And just like that, he was smiling again. As much pain as I was in, I nodded. Somehow, I managed to get up and get dressed. We worked side by side, slicing vegetables and chicken. He'd turned on music—blues. It was then I thought about what he could do with a knife.

When I got back to the dorm, I sat on my bed and cried so many tears. I felt helpless and trapped. I hurt so much—not just my body, but my heart, my soul, my spirit. I was too tired to keep going. I saw no hope. I just wanted it to end.

I wished for my family—my parents, my brothers, and sisters. I pictured that last weekend with my friends. I thought about Bobby for the first time in a long time. I knew they would all be so ashamed of me.

I decided.

I wrote a note. Nothing special. "I love you all. I'm not a good person anymore, and it hurts too much. I want it to stop."

I sat on the floor in my room, and started drinking vodka. It was easy. About halfway through the bottle, I took half the bottle of Vicodin I had left.

Sometimes I think about how easily I'd gotten it at the campus clinic. I said I was having terrible back pain, which was true, but not because I fell . . . because I got pushed. Somewhere along the way, I lost the room, the building, the earth. I floated.

I picked up the pocket knife my dad gave me when I was eight. It was my good luck charm back then. Now, it would free me. I didn't feel anything as I dragged it across one wrist and then the other. Watching the blood drip was fascinating. I wondered how long it would take. And then everything went black.

Chapter 15

BORN AGAIN

Nineteen Years Ago, November.

The first thing I saw when I opened my eyes was my dad, asleep in a very uncomfortable looking chair by my bed. He hadn't shaved and was already getting thick whiskers across his face. He wore jeans and a plaid, cotton shirt. He'd taken off his boots and I could see his white socks. Someone, maybe a nurse, had draped a blanket across him, and he had an almost useless hospital pillow folded in two under his head.

I didn't speak. I knew I was in the hospital, and it all came rushing back. I saw the IV lines pumping nourishment and health back into my broken body. My throat hurt; I guessed they intubated me.

My wrists were tightly bandaged, and I knew the stitches underneath would forever be a scarred tattoo of my failure. My mouth was dry, and it felt like my lips were cracked to the point of bleeding.

Every part of me hurt. I had a headache that throbbed continuously and made me dizzy if I turned my head too quickly. My arms hurt, and I knew I did have broken ribs. Breathing was so hard.

My stomach hurt—like someone pumped it clean, which they probably had. And everything below my waist felt battered and bruised.

Some of the pain was my own doing, I knew, but a lot of it was because of that last beating. I wondered what day it was.

Dad must have sensed I was awake.

"Hey there, honey. I'm glad you're awake. Don't talk yet. The doctor said it would be hard to do for a day or so. Would you like a sip of water?"

I nodded and he eased a straw between my parched lips. Drinking that water was a near-heavenly experience. Even though it hurt going down my throat, it was incredibly wonderful.

"Slow down, honey. The nurses said only a little, but I can get you some ice chips. That will help."

He turned to go, but I reached for his shirt. I didn't want to be alone. I needed to know my dad would keep me safe.

"Okay, okay, I won't leave. Let's just buzz the nurse."

The nurse answered.

"Mary, Victoria's awake. Do you think we could get some of those ice chips? I don't want her to drink too much water."

"She's awake! That's great. I'll be right there, and I'll bring the ice chips."

Dad sat back down and held my hand. He didn't say anything. We just looked at each other. Ever since I can remember, Dad and I communicated in a way I did with no one else. I used to joke that he and I had perfected telepathy. But sometimes it really seemed that way.

We looked at each other and knew what the other was thinking. This time, I broke the gaze and turned away. Ashamed. I closed my eyes. I was utterly and totally spent.

The nurse came in with the ice chips. She reiterated what Dad said about not talking. Told me I would be hoarse for several days. She handed Dad the ice chips, and he fed me two or three with a plastic spoon.

She checked my blood pressure, listened to my heart, took my temperature. It didn't take long. She spent more time with the data entry than it took to do the actual work of evaluating the patient.

She and Dad visited quietly, while I kept my eyes closed. Dad asked when the doctor would be coming. She told him it would be around six-thirty or seven, shortly before shift change. I knew they continued talking but I couldn't stay awake. I drifted back to nothingness.

The second time I woke up, I panicked; I didn't see Dad.

I was reaching for the nurse button when he walked in with a cup of coffee. The smell of it almost gagged me, but I didn't want him to leave. I motioned to the melted ice chips, and Dad spooned some slushy water into my mouth. I tried to talk.

"Da . . . Da . . . Dad, I'm sorry."

It came out in a raspy whisper.

"Victoria, do not be sorry. Your mom and I are the ones who are sorry. We are your parents, and we let you down. We knew something was wrong. We should have come sooner."

One lone tear fell along the right side of his face.

"I don't know what's going on, but we'll get through this together. All of us, as a family. And we shouldn't talk about it yet. I think the doctor will be here soon, and he'll help us with the next step."

He moved the hair out of my eyes and very gently kissed my forehead. And with that, my tears started, far more than one. Dad held me until only soft sighs and deep breathing remained.

Dr. Johnson was a pretty good guy, all things considered—I tried to kill myself, I was dehydrated and undernourished, and it was clear I had been abused.

The first few days, all the medical team did was attend to my physical trauma. Initially, I started with a catheter and graduated to a bedside toilet. Finally, gloriously, the actual bathroom. I was rewarded with a semi-shower and head wash on day two and never has cleanliness meant so much. More than cleaning my body, it felt like maybe it could start cleaning my soul.

They checked my stitches and rebound my wrists, not exactly hiding the damage from me but certainly working around me so I felt more than I saw.

I was up and walking the second day—initially short trips holding on to Dad, just past the nurse's station. Gradually, I worked my way up to laps around the floor.

And my appetite came back like an underfed giant. I started with broth and Jell-O. It was a feast. Soon I was ordering breakfast, lunch, and dinner from an amazingly varied and usually tasty menu. My body needed to regain strength and stability so maybe any food would have tasted great.

No one talked much about why I was in the hospital that first week. And I didn't think about it either. I blocked it. I found myself relaxing, resting, and ever grateful that my dad was with me.

No one from school or any of my friends called. I was relieved. I didn't want to talk to them or explain anything. I was cocooned and protected. Dad told me Mom wanted to come, but he convinced her to stay home and run interference for me. She called every day after I woke up. Mom's calls I could handle.

Short calls at first to tell me how much she loved me; how much everyone loved me. Later, when I could speak more clearly, we talked longer.

"So Dad tells me the food is good."

"Not as good as yours by a long stretch but it's not bad."

"If I could make you anything to eat, what would it be?"

"Easy, Mom. Fried chicken, mashed potatoes, green beans, and chocolate sheet cake."

Even as I said it, I could taste that chocolate melting in my mouth.

"Okay, you got it. And listen baby, I know you need to rest now, and get well. That's what we all want for you. But then you know, you have to tackle whatever sent you to the edge. You can't run away from it."

Mom would be the first to think, "get on with it." She talked to me about "it" before the doctors wanted. But that's my mom, and she was right. I needed to prepare. Sometimes I would wake sweating and shaking from a dream about him. I was always trapped, couldn't move, and knew he was coming to punish me—beat me—or maybe kill me. Dad knew when I had those dreams. He would wake too and get me water. Then he would rub my cheek so softly it felt like the wind and hum "It Is Well with My Soul." Eventually, I would fall back asleep.

Sometimes, during the day, I would let the old thoughts in and wonder where he was, where he thought I was, if he knew what happened to me. Dad told me one of the RAs just "had a feeling" she needed to check on me that day. She found me and called 911. She saved my life. I didn't know her but I would eventually find her and thank her. I felt certain the professor knew what happened to me. A story like mine would surely spread across campus—that girl who tried to commit suicide during Thanksgiving break. I worried at first that he might try to come and see me. But

I didn't really think he would. He would want to keep his secret.

Dad was my rock. We didn't talk much. If we did, it was nothing of importance. He talked about the rest of the family, about friends and neighbors from town, and church. And a lot of the time, he read to me. Dad has a melodious baritone voice. He read my old favorite to me, *Little Women*. I love to listen to his voice—a balm to my poor, battered heart.

After I'd been in the hospital a little over a week, Dr. Johnson came in with a woman, Dr. Mary Ann Elder. I knew before he said it that she was a psychiatrist, and I knew the reprieve was over.

"Victoria, this is Dr. Elder. You're too smart to play games, so I'm just going to tell you. She's your psychiatrist. I've done about all I can do to heal your body. You still have a ways to go, but now you need Dr. Elder to heal the rest of you."

"Victoria, I'm happy to meet you. I hope you want my help because I do want to help you."

Dad stood to the back, watching me. I didn't know what to say, and then Dad nodded to me.

"I don't know if I want your help, but I guess I need it."

"Fair enough. I doubt you will like this, but I think the way we can work the most effectively is to check you into an in-patient program at a facility here in Austin called Serenity Now."

I sat up taller and felt myself go rigid.

"I don't want to do that."

"I know. Most people don't. But think of it like summer school. You get much more done in a shorter period of time. And then, just as you think you can't do it, it's over."

I'd done summer school and could appreciate her analogy, but it didn't matter. I just wanted to go home.

"Maybe, but I really just want to go home. I'll feel so much better there, with my family. Why can't I do that and work from there?"

Dad had been listening, but he stepped forward.

"Because Victoria, home is two-and-a-half hours from Austin. It won't work. You need to get to the bottom of this. We all need to get to the bottom of this. Everyone is worried, but most of all, I need to know who has been abusing you."

I hung my head. Defeated. I would go with Dr. Elder. Really no choice. But what would I say? How could I ever tell?

Chapter 16

ALL IN THE FAMILY

Thanksgiving Day went much better than I expected. After talking to Mom and me in the kitchen, Liam hung with the guys. The women prepared the meal and served it when it was ready. Our family is nothing if not traditional. I know it sounds anti-feminist the way we do it, but that Thanksgiving, it felt like home.

After lunch, everyone scattered. Some of the guys went to watch football; they asked Liam if he wanted to join them but he didn't. Others went outside to play with the kids and work off the two and three helpings of everything we all had.

Most of the women stayed in the kitchen cleaning up or just talking. It's amazing how much my sisters and sisters-in-law can talk—about not that much. I didn't know where Liam went so I decided to look for him. After somewhat of a search, I found him in his room.

"What are you doing in here?"

"I just needed a break. That's a lot to take in—lots of people and strong personalities."

"Well, that's my family. You said you wanted to meet them. This is who they are."

"Hey, I'm not criticizing; I'm just saying I'm not used to it. I needed to check out for a while."

For some reason, it just pissed me off.

"Okay, great. Just check out. I'm going to spend time with MY family—like you said you wanted to do."

I left and didn't look back.

I decided to go outside with the boys and Derek and Christopher. Several years ago, I had a contractor build a gigantic fort with slides, tunnels, crawling spaces, and anything else I could think of—like the ones you see on a school playground. They also built a playhouse alongside it. Playhouse is kind of not really what it is. It's more like a miniature house. It has a bedroom with bunk beds, a living room/reading room, and a wraparound front porch like the big house with kid-size rockers. I'm nothing if not an overindulgent aunt . . . and kind of a kid myself. I'd always wanted a magical place, so I had this built at Mom and Dad's for the grandchildren. I doubted I would ever have children, but I loved the idea of little kids playing make-believe. And it was kind of a present to Mom and Dad too.

At the time, everyone thought it was a ridiculous idea; Gus was barely two and Franklin wasn't even born. But with two busy boys and a little girl soon to join, they begrudgingly agreed it was a great idea and would be loved by all the kids . . . and kids to come. Truthfully, the adults enjoyed playing right along with the kids.

"Hey guys, can I come up with you?" The boys were already at the top of the fort.

"Yes, Aunt Vicky, but you have to use the climbing rocks."

"Gus, is that fair? Do you think I can do that?"

"Aunt Vicky, I think you can do anything!"

Kids are so great, right? I spent several hours outside with the boys and the adults who were coming and going. At one point, William traded off with Derek so he could check on Annie and Chloe. Later, everyone came outside, and the competition began. And as evening set in, with fireflies flickering, we started running races just like we did as kids.

Liam was with us by then and seemed to be enjoying himself. I'm not sure what he did after I left him in the bedroom. It didn't matter. When he joined in, he was in a great mood.

I won every race. I'm still the fastest in the family. Running track counted for something.

Beating Christopher was the best, though. The athlete in him can't stand a loss. "Liam, your turn," he said, bent over, catching his breath.

"No . . . I don't think I want to do that."

"Chicken!" Franklin yelled. The little boys are always on my side.

"I'm not chicken, but I'm not dumb either. I've watched her run circles around all of you guys. No need for me to try." He tried to make light of it.

"Really Liam, come on," Derek tried next.

I saw Liam tense. I didn't know what he would say, so I ended the challenge.

"Nope. I've had enough. I think we all need another piece of pie. What do you say little guys? Maybe with ice cream?" I took the boys by the hands and we walked up the steps.

"Okay, but after that, we've got to head home boys," Susie said.

"No! We want to stay with Nana and Pops and Aunt Vicky!"

"Not tonight guys. You've had a big day with lots of sugar and playing and you are dirty! Go eat your pie with Aunt Vicky and Nana. We'll see everybody tomorrow."

The boys still complaining, Mom and I took them inside for the last treat of the day.

"Liam, we're going deer hunting in the morning. Do you want to go with us?" William asked. He always tries to include everyone.

"To tell you the truth, William. I've never been deer hunting. I grew up outside of Seattle, and I know how to use a gun. But I've mostly been bird hunting—duck."

"If you know how to use a shotgun, it's not that much harder to use a rifle, just different. You have to get used to the recoil, but the aim and everything's about the same. We can target practice before if you want."

"Okay, I guess. You make it sound simple, and I'll bet it isn't."

"Well, we have a saying around here, 'beginners always get the best buck.' I'll bet you do just fine."

"What do I wear?"

"I have some extra camo shirts and a cap. You can just wear jeans and use those. Dad has lots of guns. I'll let him pick one for you. So, you up for it?"

"Sure. Sounds like fun. What time are we going?"

"We usually leave around five, since we want to be set up by sunrise."

"Five in the morning? I thought we were going to target practice."

"Yep, five in the morning. Got to get up early to find the big ones. And Dad has a shooting range out by the pens. It has a light so you can take a few shots before we go."

"Okay. I guess that will work."

Derek slapped Liam on the back.

"If you're going to hang with this family, you'd better learn to hunt. Didn't Vicky tell you that even today she has one of the biggest bucks ever killed on this place?"

"No, no she didn't tell me that."

I didn't look at Liam, I just headed inside. I knew he didn't like finding out things about me I'd never told him, and he definitely didn't like the idea that I might be able to do something better than him.

After everyone left, I took a shower. Between sweat and sticky little boys with pecan pie hands, I felt gross. I put on yoga pants and a t-shirt and walked downstairs. Liam was watching the news. Mom and Dad had already gone to bed.

Before he went upstairs, I overheard Dad ask Liam, "Do you have an alarm for in the morning? I'll have coffee ready at four, some breakfast too. Since we're going to the range first, we'll do that and then meet the guys back here around five."

"Ugh . . . okay. I have an alarm on my phone. I'll set it."

"Okay, don't be late. We don't wait on stragglers."

I sat down next to Liam; I'd had a good day and was feeling generous.

"Thanks for trying so hard with everyone today. Like you said, they can be overwhelming. I'm sorry I was so short with you after lunch."

He didn't look at me.

"Now you apologize. After I'm stuck going hunting at four a.m. with the over-testosteroned men in your family."

"Hey, wait a minute. I didn't have anything to do with that. I thought you wanted to go."

"What was I supposed to do? Act like a wuss and say no thanks? You weren't even there to help me out." He was pouting, again. He was good at it.

"Don't go then. It doesn't matter. No one cares. They were just being polite. And the remark about testosterone was unnecessary." Rude and petty, more like it.

"No, I'm stuck. I've got to go. So, that means lucky you, I'm headed to bed. So I can get up at an obscene hour on my vacation."

"What do you mean by lucky me?"

"Well, it's obvious you don't want to be with me. You've avoided me all day."

"No I haven't. Most of the day, you've been pouting in your room." I knew I was taking a chance he would react badly, but seriously, he'd acted like a spoiled child all day.

"Well, whatever."

He stood and stomped up the stairs to his room and closed the door.

I sat by myself for a bit after he left. I went outside and sat on the porch swing and watched the stars. I always forget how many you can see at the ranch. It's like the sky is opening for the grand finale . . . all the fireworks come out. I don't pray much; I don't think I know how anymore. I used to pray a lot, before . . . but now I just think in my head. Is that prayer? I guess so. That night, I just thought, "Please let me get through this and get back to Boston."

Chapter 17

A TIME TO HEAL

Nineteen Years Ago, December

Being at Serenity Now wasn't much different than living in the dorm, except it always seemed like someone was watching. I don't think that's true, but with the medical checkups, therapy sessions, group meals, and room checks, I felt like a science experiment. That's how it felt in the beginning anyway.

Dr. Elder drove me from the hospital when I was released. No family was allowed until week three, just about Christmas. Someone packed a bag from my dorm room. It was nice to wear real clothes.

Neither of us said much on the drive. I appreciate that still about Dr. Elder. She doesn't feel the need to talk. And being with her in silence feels okay.

I looked outside my window and tried not to think of much. The Piano Guys played softly as we drove. Dr. Elder hummed from time to time. I wanted her to just keep driving. I felt a small molecule of peace, and I didn't want to lose it.

It didn't take long to make the drive to Serenity Now. It's up by Lake Travis, but unless you know where you're going, you'd never find it. Nothing marks the entrance—no sign, no flag. Just a turn off the highway. The driveway is shrouded in a canopy of very old oak trees. In some places, they're so thick, they block the sun. Feels otherworldly.

The driveway opens into a three-acre campus littered with the administration building, six residence halls, the main dining/meeting room, and the gym. Each residence hall has a front porch, and like all the other buildings, they're red brick with a gray metal roof. Rocking chairs and baskets of blankets sit outside.

There's a pool too, but it's closed during the winter months. It was closed when I was there.

Crushed gravel walkways wind between the buildings, connecting them together in some weird LEGO-like design. Gardens of flowers, plants, vegetables, and herbs sit off the side of the walkways—a maze of different shapes, sizes, and colors. When I was there, a few fall flowers were still blooming, mostly chrysanthemums and fall asters and herbs—thyme, mint, and sage. The garden production had almost stopped—mostly onions, cabbage, and spinach left.

I loved the pathways and the gardens and spent as much time as I could there. Tucked away in several side trails, you could find meditation benches and reading nooks. Those were my places of refuge. I've always been a reader. It provides an escape from whatever reality is ugly. The library was stocked with classics, new novels, biographies, and the self-help books they asked us to read from time to time. So I had books and a place to read. That part was probably the best.

"Well, we're here."

The car stopped in front of the administration building.

"Since your treatment is voluntary, you have to sign yourself in. There are a number of forms to complete and sign. Are you up to that?"

I really wasn't, but what else to do?

"I guess. I thought some of the information was already sent over."

"It was. What you sign now is mostly to acknowledge your agreement to be here and to follow the guidelines."

"I already read all that. You gave me copies."

"I didn't know if you would read the materials, but since you did, the rest should be quick."

I really hadn't read anything, but I figured I'd catch up on the guidelines later. Just rules anyway. And I'd figure it out. So, it was quick. Fifteen minutes and we were out the door. We stopped to get my bag and then walked down the path to the left of the admin building to the third residence hall. The sign above the entrance door simply said, "Rest."

A nice woman, maybe mid-forties, sat at the desk in the front room. She knew Dr. Elder; they visited a bit. I didn't listen. Finally, the woman handed Dr. Elder a key, and she motioned for me to follow her. We walked down a hallway and stopped at Room 8. Dr. Elder unlocked the door.

"I thought, at first, it might be better for you to have a room of your own. I wasn't sure you were up to having a roommate. Is that okay with you?"

Okay with me? Was she kidding? I didn't want to be around any people much less be confined to quarters with a stranger who was probably as screwed up as me.

"That's great."

"So, this is your room. Bed, nightstand, lamp, desk, bathroom. Nothing fancy but it should be everything you need."

It definitely wasn't fancy, but it wasn't bad either. The bed, an antique full size, was covered in what looked like a hand-stitched quilt.

On the nightstand, an antique golden oak piece, sat a Tiffany-style lamp, I'm sure a reproduction. The desk was old too, but in good shape. The chair was straight backed with a cane bottom. Not made for comfort, but still nice.

The bathroom was super clean. Nice tiled shower, sink, toilet, and pretty pale blue towels—high quality. And just like at a hotel, fluffy and inviting.

"You have most of your own personal things in your bag, but whatever you don't have and need, you can get this evening at The Store. It's a room next to the dining hall. They have toothpaste, shampoo—that kind of thing. And if you need something special, if it's approved, they'll get it for you."

"Who packed my bag?"

"I think your mother did. She and your dad went to your dorm and got all of your personal things. They took the rest home with them."

"So I guess I'm not going back to school?"

"Well, I hope you do go back. But not this semester. There's no rush. The university put you on deferred status. There's plenty of time to pick up where you left off."

"Who told the university?"

"I did. It's part of what I do for you. I try to make the outside world easier so you can work on you, and not worry."

"So, just like that, I'm good at school?"

"Well, you're not 'good, good'. I can't change your GPA or do much about your classes, but you are still enrolled and you can go back, if you want."

I sat down on the bed.

"So what happens next?"

"It's two-thirty now. Dinner is at six. So, I guess that's up to you. You can rest, you can take a walk, you can go to the library and see if there's anything you want to read."

"Where's the library?"

"You probably didn't notice it, but it's a small frame building just behind the administration building. It was an old country church, moved here about ten years ago, I think, and converted into the library."

"Don't I have to be . . . well, you know . . ."

"What? Chaperoned? Have someone monitor you?"

"Yeah, I mean. I just thought . . ."

"The staff does check on you from time to time, and we want to see you at meals and sessions, but free time is your time. And, you have about three hours of it now. Do you want me to show you around?"

"No, that's fine. I'm really tired. I think I'm going to take a nap."

"Okay. I'll be back to get you a little before six. Oh, and by the way, if you want to listen to music, I can make that happen. I like music a lot. I don't know about you."

"That would be nice. I'd appreciate that. I like music too."

"Okay, then. I'll get it done. I'll see you about five forty-five."

She left. I undressed and climbed into bed and slept without dreaming.

After that first dinner, I quickly learned the routine. Up and at breakfast by seven. First session with individual thera-pist at nine. First group session at ten-thirty. Lunch at noon. Free time until two-thirty. Second group session. Check-in with medical at four. Free time, again, until dinner at six. Large group session from seven-thirty to nine. Final free time and lights out by ten-thirty.

Weekends were slightly different. No second group ses-sion. Only large group session since it involved the outsiders. The ones who came to visit us. Usually family. You could go to church if you wanted on Sunday. Depending on what church, someone would take you to the nearest one. I didn't go to church.

You would think the strict regimen, the routine, the roteness of it all would be awful. But it wasn't. It was kind of nice to have someone else think for you. I didn't like any of the sessions at first—no one does—but once you figure out the game or once it starts making sense, which-ever comes first, it's okay.

I could go through some of those sessions with you, tell you about how we all told each other about the screwed up things we'd done. I could tell you about meetings with my therapist, Janice Williams. She was very patient and very kind—and ultimately very helpful. But, frankly, I think we've all seen enough TV shows and movies about recovery cen-ters to know how it works.

This is what I've come to believe about in-patient treat-ment: It puts life on hold. No one bothers you with details. I never even read a newspaper or magazine or watched the news while I was there. It's a time bubble. You're totally free to try to regain whatever you lost.

Some people fight it—for a long time. They resent being pulled out of the world. They don't think they need that much help. But sooner or later, if they stay, they get it too.

Others, like me, prefer to be left alone. We're happy to have the escape from real life, thank you very much, but I don't want to participate. With time, we break down the easiest. You just can't help it. The routine, the people, the stories—well, they just get to you. Eventually, almost everyone starts working to get better. Almost. A few don't. We lose them. I don't mean they died; they just leave one day, as screwed up as when they came, and usually a hell of a lot more angry. I often wonder what happens to them.

I do want to tell you about the most important day I had at Serenity Now. It was a Wednesday about halfway through my stay. By this point, I had let down my guard a bit, but I was still holding back. I participated in sessions but never told my true story. Janice and I talked a lot about everything, but I wasn't ready to open my Pandora's box.

That day it was cold, and I remember grabbing a light jacket when I left my building. I met Janice at her office in the Individual Session section of the meeting rooms.

The therapists have offices. Some of them decorate. Janice loves the beach, so her office is full of shells, dolphin figurines, sandcastles, and ocean paintings. It even smelled liked the ocean. It used to freak me out. It must have been aromatherapy. But the more I went to see her, the more I came to appreciate that smell. It eased me. I guess that was the point.

I opened the door to her office.

She has two overstuffed chairs, blue, facing each other. That's where we talked. I liked those chairs. They were big. I could sit on my legs and lay back and feel cushioned. Again, I guess that was the point.

"Hey, is it cold outside?"

"Getting there."

I took off my jacket and nestled into my chair.

"I like it when it's cold. Do you?"

"No, not really. I never seem to get warm in the winter. I'd rather be hot."

"I'm originally from Chicago, so the cold here is nothing. Have you ever been to Chicago?"

"No. My family has traveled a lot but we didn't make it to Chicago. My dad tends to like more historical cities. We've been to Washington D.C., Philadelphia, Boston, and all up the East Coast."

"That sounds great. Do you like to travel?"

"It depends. If I have to drive with my parents and my siblings, not so much. But as my dad's business grew, he had less time to drive, so we would fly. I like traveling that way."

"I bet you would like the driving if you were with someone you liked or enjoyed—not that you don't like your family, I know, but someone that you chose to go with."

"Maybe."

Instantly I thought of him. I didn't want to. I'd worked very hard not to. But I flashed to that last night when he said we would move away.

"You drifted just now. Where were you?"

I rubbed my arms, which were suddenly cold.

"Thinking about someone."

"Have we talked about this someone?"

"No. It's hard to talk about."

"Okay, hard talks usually help, but it's up to you."

I just sat. Janice waited. A few minutes later, I grabbed the Kleenex box and started the story.

Janice listened the whole time. She didn't interrupt me once. It was the best thing she could have done. I had to purge, and an interruption would have stopped the flow. It felt like throwing up. That salty taste when you know it's coming but you really don't want it to. And then you do and you feel so much better—until you puke again. But eventually, it's over and you're aren't sick anymore. Sometimes it's a twenty-four-hour bug, and sometimes it lasts several days. That day I didn't know how long it would last.

I cried a lot telling the story. I cried the hardest when I told Janice I knew I let my family down. I told her that I was scared to tell them. I said I felt like a tramp, ugly and ruined, and that no one would ever want me again. I took all the blame and gave him a clean pass.

After I stopped talking, Janice said, "I'm so sorry, Victoria. You are very brave and very strong."

I looked up, sniffling. "What? I am not. Look at what I did. I did terrible things. I lied to everyone that loves me! How can you say that?"

She leaned into me, very close. "Because you survived."

After that day, Janice helped me see that I had been a victim of a very sick man. And while he couldn't legally be classified as a pedophile, in reality, that's what he was. A much older man playing with the emotions of a very young woman—one not experienced enough to see his game.

We talked about the sexual and physical abuse. She helped me see that while I feared his anger, he had already worked to make me dependent only on him. And, that he taught me to believe his lies—to think that I was stupid; that God didn't love me.

She showed me the intricate web he weaved in pursuing me and then how he demeaned me. And, she made me realize that I knew he wouldn't let me go. She said I must have decided to take myself out of the picture completely. I think she was right on that point, for sure.

But she didn't see my attempt at suicide as weak or uncaring. She said it was the only way I knew to get away from him and the pain.

She asked me if I really wanted to kill myself when I tried. I told her that I thought I did. She reminded me that I tried on a day when I knew the RAs would be coming around to count numbers. She made me wonder. Did I just need someone else to help me get out? I'm still not sure.

We talked a lot. It was such a relief. I didn't have to keep that haunting secret anymore. But I wasn't ready to talk about it with anyone else. My heart ached for all the hurt I'd put my family and friends through. I needed to come to grips with it and find a way to forgive myself. I wanted to work on that alone or just with Janice. She was fine with it until she wasn't.

"Victoria, we've been talking about this for two weeks, every day. You are so much stronger. Can't you feel it?"

"Yes. Yes, I feel stronger, but I still have moments of fear that stop me in my tracks. And I dream about him now. I hate that."

"What do you dream?"

"Different things, but generally that he is looking for me but he can't find me."

"Do you think he is looking for you?"

I thought about that a lot. "Maybe. But probably he's hoping I will just go away. I'm sure he could get in real trouble at the university if they knew what happened."

"He would be fired."

"Do you think so?"

"Yes, and I wouldn't be surprised to find out that he abused other women before you. He's a predator."

I was stunned. I never thought of him hurting anyone but me.

"God, I never thought of that. What if he is trying to find someone to replace me?"

"I think that's very likely."

"Oh God! Oh God!"

I was shaking. Janice came and sat with me, putting her arm around my shoulders.

"You can stop him. You have the power to do that."

"What? How can I stop him?"

But I knew. I knew. I sobbed.

"I can't do it. I'm not strong enough. I don't want to see him ever again."

"I know. But if you go back to school, chances are you will—unless you stop him."

We sat there for a long time. Me crying and her holding me.

"How do I get stronger?"

"You need to tell your story to someone other than me."

"I can't. I just can't. It's so embarrassing and so humiliating."

"Remember what we said. You are not the one to feel embarrassed or ashamed. You are a victim. He is evil."

My crying didn't stop, but it eased.

"Who do I tell?"

"First, you tell your group. Strength is in that group."

"Will you come?"

"Yes. I'll come."

"Can we do it today?"

"If that's what you want, yes."

"I don't want it at all, but if I don't do it today, I may not do it at all."

"First session starts in fifteen minutes. Let's get ready."

Chapter 18

A HUNTING WE WILL GO

I didn't find out that day what happened when the guys went hunting until later that morning when Dad told me.

They'd all left the morning after Thanksgiving, very early—William, Derek, Chris, Liam, and Dad. I heard Liam as he went downstairs to meet Dad for breakfast. And I knew the plan. Short target practice and then to the blinds to get set up.

About nine-thirty that morning, the front door crashed

open and Chris came storming into the kitchen. Derek wasn't far behind. Mom and I were taking it easy, drinking coffee.

"Whoa . . . what's wrong with you guys?"

"Don't want to talk about it." Derek poured himself a cup of coffee. "Do you want a cup, Chris?"

Christopher sat down with us.

"No, I'm keyed up enough right now. Mom, what've you got to eat? I'm starving."

Mom's always prepared for the guys when they come in. She'd made biscuits and an egg and cheese casserole thing that we've all loved since we were kids. She got up and started getting the food out.

"Seriously, guys, what happened?" I tried again.

"Nothing. Nothing. Just forget about it." Chris started filling a plate. You always know when he's upset because he forgets his diet and eats whatever's in sight.

"Where's everybody else? Where's Liam?"

"They're coming. But I'm outta here before they get here." Derek downed his coffee and headed out the back door. "Chloe didn't sleep good last night. I need to go help Annie."

"Are you guys coming back this afternoon for supper?"

"I don't know. I'll see how Annie's feeling. She'll call you later."

And Derek was gone.

Something was off, wrong. I could feel it. But with Chris eating and Derek gone, Mom and I didn't know what to do.

Dad came in next. He took off his coat and hung it on the hall tree by the back door.

"How are my girls this morning?"

Dad, at least, seemed okay.

"We're good. Is Liam with William?"

"Yes, honey. They'll be here in a little bit."

"Dad, what's going on? Derek and Christopher won't talk about it, but obviously they're upset."

"I'm not upset, Vicky. I'm pissed." Chris managed between bites.

"What about? Is everyone okay?"

"Yes, honey." Dad helped himself to the biscuits. "Everyone's okay. It just wasn't a very good morning for hunting. That's all."

"That's for sure," Chris mumbled.

"Let's eat. William and Liam will be here soon. I'm sure you're starving, David." Mom, always the peacemaker.

We never got much more out of Derek or Christopher, but when William and Liam came in, there was no mistaking the tension. Liam walked in first, said hello, and excused himself to go upstairs and change. He didn't look at me, and I knew from the sound of his voice, he was upset too. I followed him upstairs.

"Liam, wait up."

He turned to me right outside his bedroom.

"What?"

That tone—I knew that tone.

"What happened? Derek blew through here like a hurricane and Chris is eating out his frustration. Everyone is obviously tense about something."

"Let's just say I don't think I'm your family's hunting type."

And he shut the door in my face. What did that mean?

Later that day, Dad told me what happened.

He and Liam met the others in the north pasture. It's densely covered with trees, and the grass is usually pretty high, especially at that time of year. It makes for good coverage for deer. We have blinds all over the ranch, but the best hunting is in that pasture. It's a family tradition to flip a coin to decide who gets the two blinds there. Dad started the story.

"It was really quiet. Still. No breeze. But it was pretty cold. We had on heavier coats and gloves. It was kind of hard to toss the coin. Liam wasn't wearing gloves. Said Boston weather made it look like spring here. Anyway, he tossed the coin. It was Derek's turn to go first, and he called it in the air. Heads. It landed heads. So Derek got one of the spots.

"Since he was a guest, we told Liam to go next. He called it before the toss. Heads. It landed heads. So, the two north pasture spots were taken. William and I picked other spots. We decided to hunt until about nine and then meet back up at the trucks.

"You know we turn off our ringers before we go to the blinds. We can text, but no sound. I'd briefed Liam on the way over about our safety rules. Don't load the gun until you're in the blind. Unload before you come down. Don't leave the blind area until time to meet. If you get a deer, text us but let it lie. We go get them after everyone checks in.

"At target practice, Liam was a pretty good shot and seemed to get the hang of the rifle, so I really wasn't worried about him with the gun. I probably should have been more cautious. I'm usually not like that. I don't know. Maybe I wanted him to feel included. For you. I really wanted to like him.

"Anyway, he and Derek left the group and headed to the blinds. Liam took the first blind, and Derek kept going to the second one.

"Like I said, it was really quiet. I remember hearing William's breath as we walked to the other pasture. It's not like he's out of shape or anything. It was just that quiet.

"We were all in the blinds by six-thirty for sure. You know how it is after that. Just watch and wait. Sometimes you kind of drift off; other times, you think you see something moving. But nothing was—not even many birds. I remember thinking it was too quiet. I expected we wouldn't get anything. Any little noise was amplified. It seemed impossible the animals wouldn't hear and scatter.

"I did see a few young doe and three or four yearlings, but nothing we would shoot. I kept listening for the others. But no one shot. The next two hours were slow. It's not much fun to hunt on that kind of morning. Maybe it was just too cold.

"Finally, about eight-thirty, I texted William and asked if he saw anything. He said nothing he would shoot. Said that Derek wasn't having any better luck. We decided to call it quits. I had Liam's number, so I texted him. Told him we were all done, that we hadn't seen anything. He texted back and said he'd really like to wait a few more minutes. He thought he'd seen a buck on the edge of the clearing south of that first blind and wanted to see if he would come out.

"So, I texted the guys and told them to wait and stay with the plan to meet at nine. No one was really happy about it, but we've all been in the same situation as Liam. Really wanting that big buck. So, we waited.

"At nine, I met William at the stock tank and started walking toward the trucks. We were just about there when we heard a gunshot. I checked my watch. It was nine ten. I wasn't sure who shot—Derek or Liam. We made it to the trucks and waited. They didn't come. We waited another ten minutes or so. They still weren't there. I got worried. So we headed into the pasture, calling for them.

"We met Derek about halfway in. I don't think I've ever seen him as angry as he was this morning.

"That son of a bitch shot at me! What the hell!? Didn't we say to leave the blinds at nine? That's what I did and just as I almost reached the first blind, he shot. I swear I heard the bullet whistle past my head. I hit the ground and yelled at him to stop. He could have killed me! Dumbass!

Liam was climbing down when I got to the blind. I asked him what the hell he thought he was doing. He had the nerve to tell me it was my fault—my fault! Said David told everyone to wait longer so I shouldn't have been walking around. I wanted to cold cock him. He's behind me somewhere. I'm leaving."

Derek was practically rambling. I know it scared him to death.

"Derek and Chris left. I told William to go back to the truck and wait for me. I went in to see Liam. And just like Derek said, he blamed Derek. And me. Said I didn't make it clear we would still leave at nine. I told him we decided to wait a bit longer at eight-thirty but that didn't change the nine o'clock stop time. He said I didn't make that clear. Then he said Derek wasn't wearing a safety vest. Said none of us were and that was careless hunting. He took absolutely no blame whatsoever for shooting at a person and by then, it was full on morning, you know, like when everyone starts back to the trucks. Honestly, there's no way he should have mistaken Derek for a deer. Maybe he wasn't wearing a safety vest but he had on an orange cap. Bright orange. I don't know how Liam didn't see it.

I think what really happened is that he wanted to prove something. He'd had a chip on his shoulder since you guys got to the house, and even Thanksgiving Day, he didn't watch the games with us. And you saw how he acted when we tried to get him to race with you.

I didn't have much to say, and I needed to stay calm. So, I asked if his gun was unloaded. He said of course it was. So, I turned around and headed back for the truck. Liam followed me."

Chapter 19

THE RECKONING

Nineteen Years Ago, December

My group was amazing. They heard my story, they loved me, they supported me, they cried with me, and they led me to the place where I could start forgiving myself. I still have to work on it. Every day. Most importantly, they told me that I had to forgive him. And, that's a whole other kind of forgiveness. I couldn't do it at first. All I felt was rage. It's still very, very hard.

Telling my family wasn't nearly as bad as I thought it would be. They all came—Mom, Dad, William, Annie, and

Christopher—the fifth weekend I was there. I didn't want them to come until after Christmas. I didn't want to ruin that special day for them, and I needed more time to decide what to say. They all sent me gifts and cards, but it was still one of the saddest Christmases I've ever had.

By the time of the family meeting, I'd spent a lot of time in session preparing, and like Janice said, I was stronger. I still worried they would be angry about the lying but, if nothing else, I've always known my family to love me pretty much unconditionally. And since everything that happened, the attempted suicide, the hospital, the obvious abuse, I thought the story wouldn't be that surprising. The person I had become wasn't their child, their sister—not like they knew her. Something really bad happened to me, and they just needed to know what it was.

We met in a private living room designed for meetings like ours. Meetings where hard things are said and heard. It was a lovely room. Bright and full of sunlight. Comfortable sofas and chairs. Beautiful paintings. Coffee, water, and tea on a serving cart. And lots of Kleenex everywhere. They were sitting down when I walked in. Janice was with me. Mom popped right up and swooped in for one of her mom hugs.

"Vicky, you look so good. I can tell you've been eating. You must be feeling better."

Mom's all about the food.

"Hey, Mom."

I hugged her back.

"I am feeling better and, yep, I got my appetite back. I have to be careful or my clothes won't fit soon. The food here is great."

Christopher hugged me next.

"I doubt that. You always could eat whatever you wanted and never gain an ounce. Just not fair. We missed you at Christmas."

We both grinned. "I know. I missed you guys too."

"Hey Will."

That day, he needed to be my big brother, Will, not William. He must have felt it too.

"Hey, Squirt. It's good to see you. Susie sends her love. She wanted to come, but we didn't know how you would feel about that."

"It would've been okay, but I know she's busy with school."

"Yeah, but this is important, too."

I hugged him tighter and held back tears. Annie just walked over to me. She didn't say a word. But as we hugged, I couldn't hold back the tears anymore. We both cried.

Then they all stepped back. Dad and I looked at each other and smiled. I walked over and held his hands.

"Thank you, Daddy, for everything."

We both knew what I meant.

"It's my job, kiddo."

"Let's all sit back down." Janice directed from that point. I sat with Dad on the couch, still holding his hand.

"I know it goes without saying that Victoria appreciates

you coming. And I know you wouldn't have it any other way. She hasn't been ready to see you until now, but I want you to know she has made so much progress. I'm very proud of her."

"It does go without saying but thank you. We are very proud of her too," Mom said.

"It's taken some work but Victoria is ready to tell you what happened to her. It's a tough story to tell, and I know it will be a very difficult story to hear. But please, just let her talk. You can ask her questions when she's ready. Okay?"

Everyone nodded. I took a deep breath and started. After I finished, Will spoke first. "Where is he? Is he still teaching?"

Janice answered for me.

"Yes, I've checked. He's finishing this semester and is slated to teach three classes next semester. And there's something else. Victoria knows this now, but she didn't until I found out and told her. He's a priest."

"What?!" My mom was shocked. Just like I had been.

Seems he was an adjunct professor at UT, but his "real" job was assistant parish priest at St. Paul Catholic Church in North Austin. That's probably why no one on campus knew he was a priest. He wanted it that way. In fact, we later learned, he specifically asked the university to list only his educational credentials, like his PhD in theology, in his bio. He told the administration he didn't want to pre-influence the students in his class with the fact he was a priest. Father Quince Matthews.

"Have you contacted the university or the church?" Will asked.

"No, Victoria didn't want to do anything until she told you."

I was amazed I wasn't crying.

"Guys, I don't know what I can do. Janice says he's a predator, and I believe that now. I'm worried that he's going to hurt someone else. But I'm kind of frozen in my tracks. And I'm scared."

"Of course you are, honey." Mom again.

Will turned to Chris, "You'll help me, right?"

"Just say the word."

"What? Wait? I don't want you guys to get involved."

Dad finally spoke. The whole time, he watched my face and held my hand. At one point, he slid his arm around me.

"Honey, we're your family. We are involved whether you like it or not. You don't have to worry about it. We'll figure it out. You don't have to do anything. Just let us deal with this. Will, who do you know?"

As it turned out, between Dad, Will, and Chris, I didn't have to do much. Dad had connections at the university, and Will had interned at the Travis County DA's office. He still knew the DA and most of the prosecutors still working there. He'd been well-liked and had been a hard worker. They were happy to help out.

Chris has always been very active in the church; even as a kid he was an altar server and super active in youth group. He played the guitar in the youth choir. Since he left home, he'd been the most faithful of all of us. Living in San Antonio, he joined Saint Matthew's and immediately jumped in with both feet there. St. Matthew's is a very powerful church in the archdiocese. And Chris knew the archbishop personally. And all archbishops know each other so contacting the higher-ups in Austin took no time.

You might say a confluence of influence meted justice to Father Quince Matthews. Just like Janice predicted, he was fired from the university. The church stood by him a little longer, but very shortly after Archbishop Silverman gave Archbishop Clary all the details, he was removed from his post and later ex-communicated. Ex-communication is extreme, but he deserved it.

The blond girl who I was so jealous of—Melissa Parks— she was his next victim. She was a freshman. She signed up for his class as an elective. He hadn't waited long after Thanksgiving. She'd already made several trips to his house by the time the criminal investigation began. She was only seventeen, a minor—a very important fact he didn't know. It made a huge difference. Whether or not she consented, he'd committed statutory rape.

He was arrested on January 24th, while he was teaching his class. As it happened, it was the Feast of Our Lady of Peace, and for me, an important day as I worked to regain my own place of peace.

As the legal process continued, I learned more about his reaction when he was arrested. He'd been greatly offended and argued with the arresting officers. I know now that is typical of sexual predators. They never see their actions as wrong, even when faced head-on with consequences. In fact, most of them admit to the action but just spin the story in a totally different way.

"What are you doing? I'm in the middle of my class. What's this about?"

From reading the police report, it was clear the officers were careful to give him the Miranda warning.

"Quince Matthews, you are under arrest for kidnapping and sexual assault. Anything you say can and will be used against you in a court of law." No one wanted to give him an easy out.

And as is also common, I've learned, predators like him often lean on their standing in the community to prop themselves up when confronted with accusations.

"Are you crazy? I don't know what you are talking about. I am a respected professor here at the university and the assistant priest at St. Paul Catholic Church. This is ridiculous."

Students in the classroom said later that even though he protested, if you looked closely, you could see his rigid façade start to crumble. Not much, but enough to know that something was off. A scandal with lots of speculation, and of course, my name, was mixed up in all of it.

Janice and I talked a lot about predators like him. There are patterns to how they behave. First and foremost, they never believe they've done anything wrong. In their minds, every act is consensual, or the act is misunderstood.

Something may have happened, but it wasn't like the victim told it. Interestingly, they rarely say nothing happened. They own their actions in some way or another. They just don't believe they did anything wrong.

Also, like Janice predicted, they are serial predators. When and if caught, it's not unusual to find a string of victims, many from years past. They're able to continue the hunt year after year because, quite frankly, the victims just want it to go away. Some lucky victims get away and build some type of life. Others aren't so fortunate.

My suicide attempt wasn't the first in Father Matthews' story either. We learned later that over his twelve years at the university, three other victims not only attempted suicide but were successful. No one ever saw the connection before. Twelve percent of college students say they think of suicide during their four years of college. About 2.6 percent actually try. The deaths of the three young women over a twelve-year period, tragic as they were, didn't reveal the true horror they endured.

Later Melissa Parks, the last victim, and I met. We were survivors of a battle. Melissa cried and hugged me and whispered, "Thank you. You saved me."

"No I didn't. We saved each other."

She was very brave. Because she was willing to testify against him, his court appointed counsel finally convinced him the risk was too great to go to trial. It took a while but he finally agreed to a plea bargain. He'd been in jail without bond for over eight months.

They asked me if I wanted to attend the sentencing hearing. I didn't. The judge sentenced him to thirty years, even though it could have been ninety-nine for the aggravated kidnapping charge alone. The DA agreed to the plea; the kidnapping would have been difficult to prove. As far as I know, he's still in prison. Will keeps up with his parole hearings. I don't think he will get out anytime soon. And he'll forever be on the Sex Offender Registry.

Melissa and I keep in touch, but I didn't meet any of the other women. Unknown to me at the time, my mom and dad made sure she got the help she needed. Her family didn't have the financial resources for it, but my parents arranged for her to go to Serenity Now. Janice was her therapist too. I'm thinking that was not a coincidence.

She's married now to a kind and generous man. They have two beautiful little girls. I'm very happy for her. She wants me to be happy too. I always tell her that I am, but by now she knows me pretty well. I don't think she believes me, but she doesn't push me either. I'm grateful for that.

I'm still working on forgiving him. Forgiveness is big. As for him—the reason he was ex-communicated—he never admitted he did anything wrong. You have to confess your sins and ask for forgiveness. 1 John 1:9: "But if we confess our sins to God, He will keep His promise and do what is right; He will forgive our sins and purify us from all wrongdoing."

Chapter 20

LIKE OLD TIMES

It was clear, even if they weren't talking, that the hunting trip was a disaster. None of them said anything, and everyone walked on eggshells to avoid the topic.

Liam came downstairs around lunch and was pleasant enough, considering everything. He helped Mom in the kitchen. He probably realized he needed an ally. Mom was a good choice. After hearing Dad's story, I couldn't be around him. I sat on the swing outside.

My phone rang. It startled me. I hadn't expected any calls. Everyone at work knew where I was, and projects were stopped until I got back. Margaret was very clear in telling me she would handle everything.

Jim and Julie and their kids went home to New York for the holiday so I doubted it could be them. Not that many other people called me. I didn't recognize the number but it was local so I answered.

"Hey, girl! We heard you were in town."

It was my best friend from high school, Clare Rogers, now Reynolds. I hadn't talked to her in—forever.

"Clare, wow! What a surprise. How are you? How's Johnny?

"We're good. We're good. The kids are in school now so life is *much* easier."

"I didn't realize that. How old are they?"

"Carrie is seven, same age as Bobby's little girl, Lee. They're in the same class. And Calum is five; he just started kindergarten. Too bad Will and Susie don't live here. I'll bet he and Gus would be best friends."

Clare always offered more answer than the question required.

"That's great. I'm glad it's going so good. You're still teaching, right?"

"Yep, middle school. It's hell, but I like the principal so that helps. I hope I can retire soon. And I get to work with Annie, so that's fun. How's she's doing? How's the baby?"

"She's great, and Chloe is precious. She's not sleeping that great, but I think it goes that way sometimes. I can't believe you want to retire. You just started teaching."

"Wrong, my friend. I've been teaching fifteen years. If I make another five, I'm done. Johnny's business is doing great so we should be okay, financially. And, I'm glad Annie and Chloe are doing good. Tell her hey for me."

"I will."

"Anyway, the reason I'm calling is to invite you and your boyfriend to meet some of us at the Stagecoach tomorrow evening. They have a great local band playing. Kevin Lasiter is the lead singer—you remember him, don't you?"

"Uh, no I really don't."

"He's about three years younger than us. He's good friends with Bobby so we all try to see him and his band whenever they play. Jackie said your mom told her you were coming to visit, so I told her I was going to make sure you came to see us."

I hadn't been around my high school friends since my freshman year at college, and I never went to any reunions. I didn't want to talk about my life or anything that happened. It was easier to avoid them all. Then I moved away and didn't have much in common with them anymore. At least that's what I told myself. Secretly, I kept up with most of them on Facebook. It made me sad sometimes,, but I couldn't see doing anything different.

"Well, geez, Clare, thanks for the offer, but I don't think we can make it."

"Why not?"

"Um, well, we leave Sunday afternoon out of Austin, so we'll need to get up early and head to the airport."

"Seriously, are you fifty years old or what? The band starts at eight. You guys can come for a while. You don't have to stay until closing, but we all really want to see you. We've missed you. You never come home and you haven't come to even one reunion. And besides, we want to meet your boyfriend. Liam, right?"

"Uh, right. And I miss you guys too, but I'm just so busy. My work is crazy. Honestly, this is the first time I've been at the ranch in a long time."

"I know. That's why I caught you. You have to come. Doug and Monica will be there. Monica is Doug's second wife. He and Mary divorced years ago. They have three of the cutest little girls. And sweet, too."

"What does Doug do now?"

"He took over his dad's farm several years ago. They're loaded, you know. Monica takes care of the kids. Oh, and of course Jackie and Bill will be there. They own the Ford dealership in town. No kids yet."

"I'm not sure I know Bill."

"Yes you do. Bill Fisher. He was a senior when we were freshmen. Quarterback, the whole thing. They got married when he graduated from A&M. Jackie didn't finish college but she helps out with the business. Actually, she's the real business mind. She has great marketing ideas. They do real well, too. Course Johnny and I will be there. And Bobby and Val. He's the superintendent now. Has been for about three years. He took over after Mr. Ridel retired. Most people think he does a good job, but it's political so someone always complains about something. He takes it in stride. You know how laid back he is. Never gets rattled. Val teaches with me. Besides Lee, they have a boy, Jackson. He's in the third grade."

Information overload. I couldn't keep up.

"It sounds like everyone is doing great. I'm glad. But, hey, I just don't think we can make it. I'd love to see everyone, but . . ."

"But nothing. You're coming. I won't take no for an answer. I'll come get you myself, if I have to. You're just making excuses."

"No I'm not."

"Victoria Jean, we may not have talked in years, but I still know you, and I know you are stalling." She softened. "Look, we all know what you've been though. You forget that we love you and we hurt for you. Don't be afraid of us. Just come and have some fun. Like old times."

She finally got me. I felt my throat tighten. I didn't want them to love me or care about me. I still didn't feel worthy. But I knew they did. It's like that with those kinds of friends.

"Okay, okay." I kind of laughed. "We'll come, but we probably won't stay long."

"That's great. Just so long as you come. It's very casual—jeans and boots, if you still have them."

"No boots, but I do have jeans. Okay, Clare, thanks for calling. I really mean that. See you tomorrow."

I hung up. So, Bobby would be there. I didn't know how that would be. Why was I being so ridiculous? He's married and has two kids. I just knew how jealous Liam had been lately. The last thing I wanted was to deal with that. I kept telling myself it would be fine.

Chapter 21

THE GREEN-EYED MONSTER

To say Liam wasn't pleased when I told him my high school friends wanted to get together at a local honky tonk is to say the British made great coffee. It isn't true. In fact, it is so not true that it's funny. At first, he refused to go.

I didn't tell him until after dinner. Everyone came, the whole family. I didn't know if they would after the hunting incident, but I was glad. I love my family so much. I was happy to see them all one more time before I left.

"You'll come back more often now, right?" Will wanted assurance. He always worries about me. Very protective.

"Yes, I think so. I have to admit it's been great to be back at the house, at the ranch. Yep, I'll be back."

"Great. Spring will be beautiful. We've had a lot of rain this winter already and more coming. The wildflowers will be outstanding," said Chris's wife, Jennifer. She and I shared a love of plants and animals.

"It's been a long time since I've seen a bluebonnet."

Dinner conversation was easy. We told stories about our childhood. Laughed about things Mom and Dad didn't know—or at least we thought they didn't know. Liam even told a story or two. Everyone was on their best behavior.

The food, as usual, was the best. Like I'd requested years ago, Mom made my favorite. Fried chicken, mashed potatoes, and green beans. Instead of cake, though, it was banana pudding for dessert.

Everyone ate too much, and after dishes, it was time to say goodbye.

I hugged everyone and smothered the little boys in kisses. Franklin loved it, but Gus wiped them off.

"Hey, mister, don't rub off my kisses or no more presents for you!"

He laughed and jumped into my arms for a bear squeeze.

Derek and Annie were spending the night at the ranch so I would have more time with Chloe. I'd grown so attached to her, even in three short days. I loved her smell and her sweet little mouth. You could tell she would be beautiful.

She had Derek's dark hair and Annie's light complexion. She'd complain as she grew up about being so fair. We all did, but she would be beautiful. It goes without saying she would be smart. Smart is in her blood.

After the others left, I helped Annie give Chloe a bath.

"Annie, Chloe is the sweetest baby ever."

Annie smiled a mother's smile.

"I know. I'm so lucky. I have to pinch myself. She doesn't always sleep all night, but that's okay. She's such a happy baby."

"Sometimes I wish I had kids, but I don't think it's in the cards for me."

"Why do you say that?" Annie wiped her hair out of her eyes with her elbow and helped Chloe in the bubble bath.

"I think that time has passed. I'm married to my work now, and I don't expect that to ever change."

"What about Liam?"

"What about him?"

"You don't see staying with him, maybe having kids?"

"Nope. Mom probably already told you, but Liam and I are basically over. I just need to get back to Boston and make it official."

She stopped what she was doing and turned to me.

"No, honestly Mom hasn't said anything. But I can't tell you how relieved I am. You can do much better."

"I don't know about that, but I just know this isn't right for me. Lately he's gotten really jealous. I can't stand it. I know I could never live with anyone like that."

"And he's a prick."

"What do you mean? Did Derek tell you something?"

"Let's just say, we'll all be glad to see the last of Liam."

I knew Liam didn't fit in, but until then, I didn't realize how much they all disliked him. I felt like I had to apologize. But I didn't know what to say.

Chloe finished her bath. We both concentrated on her. She was in her pj's and to bed before seven. After that, I couldn't put it off anymore. I went to find Liam.

He was sitting on the front porch reading. He looked up and smiled when I sat down beside him.

"Whatcha reading?"

"Just a novel I picked up at the airport."

"Is it good?"

"Good enough to hold my attention. Did you ladies get Miss Chloe to bed?"

"She's bathed and in pj's. Annie's feeding her now. She'll be asleep soon."

"I like her, don't you?"

"Who, Annie? Of course. She's my sister."

"No, Chloe. Wouldn't you want a little Chloe someday?"

Time to change the subject. It was so far beyond my reality that there wasn't anything to say. It wasn't the best timing, but I needed to tell him about Clare's call.

"Well, I don't know . . . but, hey listen. One of my old friends from high school, Clare Reynolds, called this afternoon. Several of my high school friends are getting together this evening to listen to some live music. They want us to come."

"I thought you didn't want to have anything to do with your high school friends."

"It's not that I don't want to have anything to do with them; I just don't have much in common with them anymore." And I knew small-town gossip. There was no way everyone in six counties didn't know my college story—even though it had been almost nineteen years ago. It was the main reason I avoided coming home. Being a victim is bad enough, but having everyone think they know your story is worse. You either get pity or scorn. I didn't want either.

"So, what's changed? Do you want to go?"

"I'm not sure, but Clare threatened to come and get us herself if we didn't. She would do it too. I tried to beg off telling her that we have to leave for the airport early tomorrow, but she called my bluff. Said we were acting like old people."

"And so, we are going, even if I don't want to, right?"

"No, we don't have to. I wanted to ask you first."

"Really? Do you? Do you really want to ask me first? It seems to me I don't really have a choice, do I? You've already committed. Who's going to be there?"

I repeated as much as I could remember from Clare's description of everyone.

"So, your old high school boyfriend, the guy that broke your heart, he's going to be there?" That jealous undertone.

"He didn't break my heart. He was just my first real boyfriend. We've talked about this already . . . several times. And yes, he'll be there. But you know he's married and has two kids. Besides, that was just a high school thing. I haven't seen him or thought about him in forever. It's just the old gang. It's no big deal."

"No big deal, huh? I don't think so. Maybe you asked Clare to call and invite you—or us?"

"What? No! I don't even have Clare's phone number. I didn't even recognize the call."

"So how'd she get it?"

"Get what?"

"Your . . . phone . . . number."

Like I was a moron.

"Oh, Mom gave it to her last week."

"Convenient."

"Liam, you are making a big deal out of nothing. If you don't want to go, we don't have to. I can get out of it. I'll just wait until later and call Clare. If she's already there, she won't leave to come get us." I didn't want to argue, and I didn't really think it was a good idea to go anymore anyway.

"Oh no." Sarcastic. "Oh no, we're going. I want to see what's really going on."

"You are crazy. There's nothing going on."

He grabbed my arm—too hard.

"Do not ever tell me I'm crazy. I am not crazy. Do you hear me?"

"Yes, I hear you. Please let go. That hurts." He did.

"What time and where?"

"Eight or so at a place called the Stagecoach."

"It's seven fifteen. I'm going to get ready. I'll be back down at seven forty-five."

And he left.

Something was too familiar. My arm hurt where he squeezed it, but it wouldn't bruise. He'd been kind of rough with me in the last couple of months, but he never physically hurt me. I doubled over my stomach hurt so much. I needed to find my purse. It was only the second time since we came home that I needed the pills.

We left at seven forty-five. Liam was in a good mood. The roller coaster of his emotions was wearing me out. I didn't know what to expect or when something would change.

The music was already playing when we walked in the front door. The Stagecoach is an old dancehall that's been around since the 1920s. It hasn't changed much. Wood floors, bar in the back, tables scattered around the stage and a big dance floor.

We all grew up going to the Stagecoach for Saturday night dances. And we all loved to dance. The only real change I could tell was the air conditioning and no smoking inside. Hooray for both.

Clare spotted us before I saw her. She waved from a table near the back. We weaved our way through the dance floor.

She immediately grabbed me and jumped up and down. Did I mention she was a cheerleader when we were in school?

"I'm so glad you came. I didn't know if you really would."

"Did you give me a choice?" I grinned. "I couldn't have you driving out to the ranch and fussing at me."

The music was loud, and it was always hard to hear in

the Stagecoach. You either talked very loudly or you talked directly into a person's ear. Clare talked really loud. She turned to Liam and smiled.

"You must be Liam. I'm so happy to meet you. I'm Clare Reynolds."

"Hi Clare. Vic told me a little about you. It's great it worked out that we could spend some time with her old friends."

I couldn't even look at him. So sanctimonious.

"Let me introduce you to everyone else. Guys . . . look who's here!"

Of course, they'd already seen me, and several had waved or mouthed "hello." I waved back.

"This is Liam. Liam, what's your last name?"

"Nelson."

"Liam Nelson. Vicky's friend from Boston."

Everyone said hi or gestured in some way in acknowledgment.

"Let's walk around the table." While Clare made the rounds with Liam in tow, I sat down beside Jackie.

"Hey, Vicky. How are you? It's great to see you, finally. We've all missed you."

Clare, Jackie, and I were known as "the trio" in high school. We hung out all the time, went on dates together, and got in lots of trouble together. Nothing bad, harmless really compared to kids today, and we always managed to get out of it. Our parents raised us as a tribe. Mrs. Rogers, Clare's mom, was just as likely to dress me down as my own mom. The parents gave each other permission to treat each kid as their own. And they did.

"I'm sorry. It's been hard. I . . . uh . . . didn't want to see you guys for a long time. You know—I'm sure the gossip was crazy. I didn't want to talk about it then and I still don't. And besides, now work is crazy busy."

She squeezed my hand. She smelled like lavender—same perfume as high school.

"Well, you're here now, and that's all that matters. Want something to drink?"

I hadn't planned on drinking, but my nerves were raw, and I'd already taken two pills. A bit risky but nothing I hadn't done before.

"Sure. How about a Corona?"

"Great. Bill. Vicky, you remember Bill?"

"Honestly, Bill, I don't. But I'm told you were a senior when we were freshmen."

"Yep, that's right."

He still looked like a high school quarterback. He must have worked out every day. I'll bet he even had a six-pack.

"All us senior guys eyed you freshmen girls, but you were kind of off-limits. Not anymore." He gave Jackie a kiss on her cheek.

"He always says that about us being off-limits." Jackie smiled at him. I was envious. They seemed to like each other.

"So, honey, would you get us a beer? We both want Coronas, with lime."

"As you wish, my lady!"

He got up and headed to the bar.

"He seems great."

She watched him a minute.

"He is. I'm very lucky." She turned back to me. "So tell me about Liam."

And that's how much of the night went. One by one, they all came and sat with me. Each one said it differently, but the message was the same. We love you. Why didn't you trust us enough to let us help you? We want you back. What about Liam?

Several times I teared up. But the beer helped. They kept buying, and I kept drinking.

They each spent time with Liam too. I don't know what was said, but I'm sure they welcomed him. They would do that anyway 'cause that's the kind of people they are. But I knew they were doing it more for me.

Liam was in his element. I heard him telling stories I'd heard a million times, but he got laughs. And they were buying him drinks too. Not beer but scotch. I worried at first. Sometimes Liam isn't nice when he drinks, but I was buzzed and worrying about him didn't seem to matter after a while.

I danced with Doug. At the same time, Monica took Liam by the hand, him protesting with a grin, and walked him around the dance floor. Actually, credit where credit is due, Liam can dance. He just hadn't danced country western. Monica was a good teacher and he caught on. He and I danced the next dance.

"Are you having fun?" I talked in his ear.

"Surprisingly, yes. That Monica is great. I really like her."

"She seems like it. I don't know her. She's Doug's second wife. I only knew his first wife."

"First wife must've been a bitch. He's got a keeper now, though."

I didn't respond.

"How much have you had to drink?"

"What do you care?" Immediately defensive.

"I don't. I'm just trying to decide which of us will be the DD."

"Don't worry about it. I'm driving."

The song ended and he left me standing alone on the dance floor and went back to the table—to sit by Monica.

Bobby walked up to me just as the music started again.

"Hey, I haven't had a chance to talk to you. Want to dance?"

He caught me off guard.

"Sure."

I wasn't nervous exactly but I was hyperaware of everything. The music, the crowd, my friends watching us, his wife watching us. Liam watching us.

It was as natural as breathing air—dancing with him again. How many times had we danced when we were in school together? Hundreds. I tried to calm down, but it was hard. I wondered how he felt.

"So, I hear you're a big, successful business executive these days."

"Umm. I guess so. I've done okay. It's a great job, even if it seems like the only thing I do."

I hadn't meant to complain. But if nothing else, Bobby and I had been great friends. He always listened to me, heard me, and usually gave me pretty sound advice. I like to think I did the same for him.

"You always were driven. We all knew you'd outrun us."

"That's stupid. I didn't outrun anybody. If anything, it seems to me that all of you guys are pretty happy, Mr. Superintendent."

I could tell he smiled even though we weren't looking at each other.

"Yes, we are happy. But you know happy isn't a constant state. You get it from time to time, but every day you strive for content."

"I'd take content."

"You're not?"

"Yes and no. I do like my job, but I don't seem to have any of those ups and my content is more like catching up on sleep whenever I can."

"That's sad."

We danced. I wanted to close my eyes, just to rest for a minute. But I knew that would cause a stir. We were in the old fishbowl, every movement, gesture, and expression being analyzed by someone, if not everyone.

"What if you could change things? What would you do?"

I wasn't sure where he was going.

"I haven't thought about it. I'm just doing."

"What about this guy, Liam? Do you love him?"

I should have stopped the conversation then.

"No. No, I don't."

"Then why is he here?"

"Good question. The truth is because I'm a coward. I need to end it but he wanted to come to Texas so much. I didn't have the heart to say no."

"And now?"

"And now, since I've been home, since I've been back at the ranch, I know it's the first thing I'll do when I get back."

The song ended. We smiled at each other and waved to the table. No big deal guys.

But it was a big deal. As soon as I sat down, Liam came and sat by me. He was on at least his fifth drink. It was hard to tell with him unless you'd seen it, but he was drunk. And drunk Liam could go several ways. This time, he was leaning toward angry.

"Are you trying to embarrass yourself—and me, by the way?" He hissed in my ear.

I just looked away. I wasn't in the mood for a fight so I didn't say anything. He grabbed my face and forced me to look at him.

"Did you hear me? What are you doing, trying to hook up with the old flame?"

"Liam, please let go of me."

He didn't.

"You need to answer me. You still have the hots for ole Bobby?"

"Liam, that really hurts. Please stop. Bobby's just a friend."

By this point, his grip had tightened.

"Just a friend, my ass. How long has this been going on? Is this why you wanted to come home?"

He was drunk and totally irrational. Nothing I could say. I was in tears, not only from the pain in my jaw but from the shame, the embarrassment—everyone was watching. The band had taken a break so suddenly every word spoken was heard loud and clear.

I tried to push his hand away, but it was a death grip. And then his head snapped back and he let go. I looked up to see Bobby delivering a second punch.

Everyone closed ranks around us so the rest of the crowd couldn't see. Liam jumped up ready to fight but Doug held him back. Johnny held onto Bobby. I didn't know what to think or do.

Liam reached down and picked up my purse.

"Come on, Vic. We're leaving."

I saw the look in my friends' eyes. They were scared for me. Clare whispered, "Stay with us. We'll take you home."

But I shook my head. I had to go with him. I was humiliated and just wanted to block it all out. And besides, I didn't know what would happen if I didn't go with him.

I pointed to the back door and motioned to Liam to leave that way. He walked out and I followed. We got to the car. Even though he was too drunk to drive, I knew better than to stop him. I just prayed we made it home.

He didn't say a word the whole drive, and miraculously, we made it.

Chapter 22

THE OTHER SHOE

He cut off the engine and turned to me. I saw pure hate in his eyes. But he still didn't say anything. It was late—about twelve-thirty when we went in. The house was quiet. I headed upstairs to my room. I just wanted to wash my face and sleep. As I reached my bedroom door, Liam shoved his way in.

He grabbed me and threw me on the bed. He covered my mouth with his hand.

"So, you think you'll get away with it again, huh? I'll bet that old priest didn't know who he was up against. Everyone thinks 'Poor little Victoria. All the men are so mean to her.' But that's not true, is it?"

I could smell the sour scotch. I gagged.

"That's not true, right, Vic?"

He slapped my face, hard. The bed cushioned the blow but the sound was too familiar. And this time it would bruise.

Like Alice, I started falling back down the rabbit hole.

"Liam, please stop, and please be quiet. You're going to wake up everyone."

"And do you think I care?"

I guess he didn't because he got louder and louder. He slapped me again.

"You are nothing but a prick tease and a whore. You need to be taught a lesson once and for all."

I screamed into the bed. The more I screamed the harder he pushed my head into the bedspread. I had to stop just to breathe. It was a battle. I tried not to cry. I needed to breathe. I felt like I was dying. Maybe I was.

Bang!

He fell on top of me. Dead weight. I pushed him away and scrambled off the bed. I watched as my bedspread turned from blue to red. It didn't make sense. I tried to reason through it, but I couldn't.

And then Dad pulled me out of the room. Mom was standing with the rifle in the doorway.

I saw Derek take the gun from Mom. Then he went into the bedroom.

"Derek, he's dead." Mom said. "You can check. But he's dead."

"David, what do we do now?" Derek stopped.

"Call William. Then call Sheriff Patterson. Then call 911. Where are Annie and Chloe?"

"In the bedroom." Derek was surprisingly calm.

"Take them home and then come right back. I'll need your help. And call Chris on the way. Ask him to come too."

"I'll go make some coffee. It's going to be a long night." As Mom walked downstairs, she stopped and turned around. "And Derek, do not wipe down that gun. Leave my finger-prints right where they are."

I couldn't believe what happened. I'm sure, looking back, I was in shock. Dad helped as I tried to catch my breath, and then it all went black.

I woke up in my parents' room. Jennifer was sitting with me. She came when Chris did. She smiled when I opened my eyes. I didn't know what was happening at first and then I remembered the blue turning to red.

"I'm going to be sick."

She helped me to the bathroom. We made it in time. I puked and puked until nothing was left. She stayed with me, handing me tissues, wiping my forehead with a wet cloth, telling me everything was alright.

When it was over, I sat back on my knees, still shaking.

"Where are Mom and Dad?"

"Everyone's downstairs."

"How long was I passed out?"

"Not long. Maybe thirty minutes, not much more."

"What's happening?"

I couldn't move. Frozen and cold. Jennifer went to the bedroom, grabbed a quilt, and wrapped it around me.

"Don't worry. You're just in shock. You're going to be okay."

I wondered if that was true.

"I need to go downstairs."

"No, you need to stay here. You need to rest."

"Jennifer, really, I'm not a baby. I need to go downstairs."

She sighed. "I told them I couldn't stop you. Okay, I'll help you."

As I stood up, I glanced in the mirror and saw the beginning of two black eyes. My old friends.

We hobbled into the kitchen and everyone stopped talking. Mom and Dad were there. William, Derek, Christopher, and Sheriff Patterson. No one seemed particularly upset but they were worried about me.

Chris stood up. "Sit here, sis."

He took me from Jennifer and helped me to the chair. I didn't realize how much I hurt.

"Honey, do you need something to drink?" How could Mom be so calm?

"No, Mom. I don't need anything to drink. I need to know what's going to happen now."

Sheriff Patterson spoke up. "I'm very sorry about your loss, Victoria. Your family's been telling me about how troubled Liam was."

What was he talking about?

"No one knew he kept the rifle your dad loaned him. I'm sorry you had to find him like that."

What did I miss? Mom shot Liam. What was the sheriff telling me? I looked around the room. Everyone met me with clear eyes.

"David, Carolyn, as soon as the coroner's finished, we'll be done. Shouldn't be much longer. My office will notify Mr. Nelson's parents. I'm sure they will want to make arrangements for the body."

And with that, he stood up, tipped his hat, and walked out.

Dad spoke calmly. "Victoria, it doesn't matter what you think you saw, Liam shot himself. He was very drunk and was still upset over what happened when we were hunting yesterday. I know you were drunk, too. Clare and Jackie said you both had a lot to drink at the Stagecoach. When you came home you went into your old room by mistake and fell asleep. Maybe you didn't even hear the gunshot."

"I heard the gunshot. I SAW the blood."

"I know, Vicky, I'm sorry I couldn't stop you," Derek said. "We didn't want you to see."

"What is going on? Am I the only one that's hallucinating here?"

"Sweetheart, you aren't hallucinating. If you stop and think, you'll remember it all," Mom said. "You'll remember how much your family loves you, how much your parents love you, how much I love you. And, you'll remember we are always going to protect you."

It started to make sense. But I still didn't understand why everyone was pretending Liam shot himself. Mom was just defending me, right?

William picked up. "We've known Sheriff Patterson since we were kids. Remember how he caught Annie and Derek making out on Outback Road?" He smiled sadly. "Sheriff Patterson is a friend. And he's one of us. We all help each other out in this part of the country. It's a sad thing that Liam is dead, but it's no one's fault but his own. You are not to blame. Mom's not to blame. And we want to keep it that way. There's no reason anything else needs to happen."

Everyone waited for me to speak.

"I need to go back to Serenity Now for a while. I hope Janice is still there."

And that was that. The official cause of death: suicide by gunshot. I didn't ever understand how they pulled it off. How was it believable? Why didn't Liam's family question it? I'm sure no one would have found Mom guilty. But, just like once before, my family connections smoothed the bumpy surface.

Chapter 23

NO MORE LIES

I need to confess. I lied to you at the start of this story. Maybe lie is too harsh a word to use. But I wasn't wholly truthful. I told you all about my wonderful life, how rich I was. I wanted you to believe my life in Boston was perfect. I wanted you to think I'd made it in the world, that I was special. Maybe I wanted to believe that, too. But, as you see, my life wasn't perfect. No one's is. I'm sorry. I misled you. I hope you will forgive me.

I sometimes wonder now, after all that happened, why so many bad things happened to me. I know bad things happen to everyone. I know others have terrible stories, circumstances, and experiences worse than mine.

I count my blessings: my family, my friends, financial freedom, support from so many people—basics like a roof over my head, food, air to breathe, clean water to drink—very, very basic blessings. I understand how lucky and fortunate I am. Intellectually, I understand. Emotionally, I continue to struggle. I know healing is a journey. I try to be patient and let it come. Some days are easier than others.

So how does my story end? I guess we'll see. Here's what happened after Liam was killed.

While I was at Serenity Now the second time, Dad and Will went to Boston and shut down my life there. I asked them to do it. The talked to my company. They arranged for the sale of my properties, my cars, everything. I told them to sell it all. I only wanted a few things—mostly things I took with me from home.

They delivered letters to Margaret and Jim and Julie. I included sizeable checks. I didn't want them hurt by my leaving. I haven't gone back to visit. Margaret came to see me, and I keep in touch with Jim and Julie. Their son is getting married next year. I hope to go. For now, it brings me peace to know they are doing well.

When everything was finished in Boston, it was clear I never really needed to work again. My investments are more than enough to allow for a very nice life. The buildings alone had almost tripled in value, clearing a ridiculous amount of money when they sold.

And, I had the money from the Catholic Church. Back

then, Will had decided, despite Chris's protests, to make sure the church was punished for protecting Father Matthews, even if it was only for a short time. With the help of several other lawyers, a lawsuit was filed on behalf of Melissa and me. Initially, I wanted to leave it alone; we'd all been punished enough. Then I realized the money was important to Melissa, and ultimately her family. And, Will was right. Evil can't thrive in the light. The lawsuit provided one more opportunity to shed light on a very ugly subject.

We didn't go to trial. The church didn't want or need any more publicity, especially in light of allegations of abuse against other priests. After some legal back and forth, we reached a settlement. A sizeable one.

I didn't stay long at Serenity Now the second time. After six weeks, Janice started pushing. She and I both knew I was okay. I needed to reinforce what she taught me before, but I still knew the questions AND the answers.

"So, Victoria, what comes next?"

"I really don't know. I don't want to think about that now."

"Well, I'm sorry, but you have to."

"Why? As long as I'm paying, why can't I stay here?"

"Because it's not healthy. Our job is to get you ready for the next part of your journey. And that doesn't mean hiding here."

"I'm not hiding."

"Okay, then, why won't you see your friends? Clare, Jackie, Doug, even Bobby. They all want to come see you."

I stared out the window, smelling the make-believe ocean.

"I'm such a loser. How can I face them?"

"If you keep this up, I'm going to stop talking to you."

"What? Keep up what?"

"The pity party. Have you had some really bad things happen to you? Yes. Was it your fault? No. Will something bad happen again? Maybe. But, are you a loser? Absolutely not. And we have been over this time and time again."

"I know. I know. I just need a little more time."

"Well, then, see your friends. Decide what comes next. Do something good for the cause. Start back on your journey."

"Do you think I'll make it?"

"Depends on where you want to go. But I know staying here won't get you anywhere. You have to leave. This isn't the real world, and you know that."

She was right. I was feeling sorry for myself. I wanted to see my friends—at least Clare and Jackie. I'd call them, and I knew they would come.

"Okay, give me another week. I promise this time next week, I'll be ready."

"One week. I'll hold you to it."

Turns out, I didn't stay the week. I left the day after my session with Janice. I'd known it was time to go. And Janice was right. I'd learned about predators and how they worked years ago. But, Liam wasn't really a predator, not in the same way as I experienced before. He was just a messed up guy who had too many issues of his own that he wouldn't or couldn't face. I realized I'd known very early on that our relationship was off. I remembered the creepy feeling I got when we rode up in the elevator together . . . the day he asked me to the ballgame. But I wanted to be "normal" so badly that I ignored so many warning signs. That's what Janice and I talked about the most this time—trusting my instinct, listening to my inner voice, knowing I could protect myself.

I had no way to ever thank Janice for all she did for me—pulling me back from the brink—twice. But afterward, I tried. I bought a comfortable, restful beach house on South Padre Island, and I gave it to her. At first, she refused. She said it would be unethical. I told her to do with it whatever she wanted. She could sell it and give the money to Serenity Now, if she wanted. After soul-searching and discussions with management at Serenity Now, she kept it. She goes there as often as she can, and I go with her from time to time. It helps both of us.

My family recovered, mostly. It took time for everyone to find the new normal. Will concentrated on his work, and he had Susie and the boys; that's how he coped.

Derek struggled the longest. He felt he should have been the one to help me that night—not Mom. No one else, especially Mom, felt that way. Things worked out because it was she who stopped Liam. Derek had Annie and Chloe to consider. He finally started counseling, and he's getting better.

Christopher and Annie each coped in their own way. I think all the secrecy affected Chris more than we knew at the time. He lost his way with the church for a while. Eventually, when John David was born, he regrouped. He and Jennifer moved home and live in Mom and Dad's first house on the ranch. Jennifer works as the school nurse. It gives her more time with JD. Even though she's never talked to me about it, I know that night and everything afterward took its toll on her. She's strong, though. Kind of like Mom. The changes they made have been good for them.

Annie and I talked often in the first few months afterward. She came to see me at Serenity Now the first week I was there. She even stayed with me a few days. We had to get special permission, but between Janice and Dr. Elder, it wasn't really a problem. She didn't see what actually happened, and Derek took her and Chloe to their house right away. She didn't have any mental images of that night to try to erase. Mostly, like Derek, she felt guilty. I understand that. It's not that different from survivor's guilt, as I've been told. Survivors aren't sure why they were spared when someone else died, so they feel guilty about it. She started counseling with a therapist in San Antonio recommended by Janice. And she's busy with her kids. In April, about a year and a half after that night, baby Rosie was born. She is as precious as Chloe. All the children—Rosie, Chloe, JD, Gus, and Franklin, well, they give us such great joy—and hope.

Guilt seemed to be the ghost in the air after that night. Dad felt guilty, too. He feels guilty over lots of things. He didn't come and get me at UT. He didn't see the danger lurking inside Liam. He didn't protect me. When we talk about it, and we rarely do, I remind him I pushed them away and was a very convincing liar. And, that no one saw what was coming with Liam—except maybe me. I'd had signs but I ignored them because I never believed I would be in the same situation twice. I don't want Dad to feel guilty; all I can do is reassure him.

Mom, well, she's still the rock. Of course, she was upset. Who wouldn't be after what happened? I don't know if she felt remorse. She did go to confession. But she feels justified in her actions and believes, without a doubt, she saved my life. She may be right. I pray I find her wisdom and strength.

My friends have been wonderful. I've reconnected with all of them, even Bobby. Clare and Jackie and I have a standing girls' night out every two months. Sometimes it's a weekend. Last time we invited Bobby's wife, Val, and Doug's wife, Monica. We spent the weekend in Comfort at a lovely bed and breakfast that backs up to the Cypress Creek. It's quiet and peaceful. The property is peppered with different houses that have been moved onto the site. Now they can be rented and come with the use of a smaller screened in house for visiting, reading, or playing board games. There's a small pool and breakfast each morning served in the great room. After that breakfast, you don't really need to eat again until dinner. It was a nice weekend. We don't ever talk about what happened that Thanksgiving, though. It's over for us, and we look ahead.

And me? I struggled for a long time. I went back to the ranch after I left Serenity Now. Mom and I redid parts of the house, including Annie's old room. We needed to change the memories. I stayed at the ranch until after Rosie was born. Then I knew it was time to move on.

What do you do when you don't know what else to do? You go to law school. So that's what I did. I went back to UT. With my LSAT scores and my other degrees, I got in easily. Those three years were good for me. Law school is hard. So much reading. It takes all your time. It consumed my life, which was good. Even when it was over, studying for the bar exam kept me preoccupied.

During law school, I volunteered at the DA's office, and I loved it. But I realized quickly that any kind of litigation wasn't for me. I never saw myself being a prosecutor. I didn't mind the actual courtroom, but all the work to get there was too much. And, I hated the delays.

I didn't interview for jobs while I was in school, even though several larger firms tried to recruit me. I never thought much about life after law school. In a way, it was another shelter from reality. But, after taking the exam, I got stuck again.

Shortly after I finished the bar, Janice asked me to co-author a book with her. She wanted to write about the connection between domestic violence and suicide. She'd done extensive research and wanted to include my story. I hesitated at first, but then I remembered Melissa. I decided if my story saved one person, it would be worth telling.

The book was a success. *The New York Times* Best Seller list. No one was more surprised than Janice and me. Janice became a true celebrity, and I became a kind of minor one.

Janice was asked to speak to groups all across the country about her research and domestic violence. Most of those groups wanted to hear from me too.

If you remember, I'm not an extrovert, but, amazingly, I found talking to those groups was easy. For the most part, they were women like me or educators helping women like me. I was comfortable with them.

Now, Janice and I travel throughout the year, attending different events. We've even been asked to speak at the National Health Resource Center's National Conference on Health and Domestic Violence. We don't charge for our time. The settlement money from the church serves a noble purpose. We use it for our expenses and find ways to quietly give it away.

My home is in Austin now. I've made a few new friends here. I volunteer at the SAFE Children's Shelter and I spend a lot of time outdoors. I find God is easiest to find when I'm in His bigger world. I've learned to kayak and spend several days a week on Lake Austin like so many others.

On free weekends, I'm part of a hiking club. We do day-trips around Austin and spend the day walking and sometimes climbing.

I'm still not married, but I've been on some dates. I feel healthy again. I'm ready to try. I don't dwell on it, but, in my heart, I haven't given up. I think, whether we accept it or not, we were made to find our "other." We yearn for that connection. I do, anyway. God willing, I'll find it.

AUTHOR'S NOTE

In writing this book, my main purpose is to help abused women and those considering suicide to realize that there is help, a way out of seemingly hopeless situations. I also want abused women of all ages, including children, to know that abusers can be held accountable. The legal system does work, and more and more, it is protecting and supporting the abused. I hope that everyone reading this book understands that sexual, physical, and emotional abusers won't be stopped until someone stops them. These predators do not change. They are, in almost every instance, serial predators. They abuse over and over. It takes courage and support to confront the evil of abuse, and we need courage.

In this story, Liam is killed. I do not in any way condone or suggest that violence of this type is a solution for abuse; It is not. The death of Liam was a plot twist, only, to capture the attention of the reader.

In the If You Need Help section, I have included information on groups that offer help and guidance to those in life-altering situations like those described in this book. Please use them.

It is my prayer that at least one person will seek care and refuge because of reading this book. If only one person is helped, then I will consider this book a success.

Let us all continue to hope. No matter the circumstances, there is a way to a better place, a better life—with time and support.

ACKNOWLEDGMENTS

I would like to thank my children, Anthony, Erin, Carly, and Bethany, of whom I am immensely proud. They have always encouraged me, believed in me, and loved me no matter the situation. I've also been so blessed with the most precious grandchildren—Evelyn, Henry, Oliver, and James. My hope is the lessons of this book create a better world for them.

I would also like to acknowledge my extended family and friends, too many to name, but hopefully you know who you are. Your unwavering love and encouragement are a constant source of inspiration.

I would be remiss if I didn't also thank God for leading me along this path. Even when I wanted to stop, He pushed me on. Whatever the outcome, I hope that I have fulfilled His purpose.

I also want to express my respect and admiration for

all the women and men who have been though experiences similar to the ones described in this book. This book was conceived before the #MeToo movement, but I am hopeful it provides additional information to address the issues of sexual abuse and its aftereffects so that we, as a society, will continue to right these wrongs. My utmost respect and admiration for those who are willing to tell their own stories—they are courageous and determined. Thanks, as well, to the prosecutors and others in law enforcement who don't turn a blind eye, but rather act to stop predators.

Finally, much gratitude is also owed to my team at Greenleaf Book Group, Daniel Sandoval, Lindsay Bohls, Sam Alexander, Tiffany Barrientos, Lindsey Clark, Teresa Muniz, and Chelsea Richards, who believed in me even when I doubted myself, and helped make this book so much better than it would have ever been without them.

QUESTIONS FOR DISCUSSION

1. We learn early in the book that Victoria's relationship with the professor is not only wrong, but also abusive. Does knowing this early in the story create anxiety as you watch the relationship progress? Why or why not?

2. Victoria is clearly a cautious person, especially in relationships, given her past. Is this caution understandable and/or relatable? Do you think she could have put herself out there more over the course of the nineteen years?

3. What did you make of Victoria and Liam's relationship initially? Did you expect Liam to show signs of possessiveness and eventually abuse?

4. What are some of the differences between Victoria nineteen years ago and Victoria today? Do you think some of these differences are signs of growth, coping, both, or something else?

5. Was it difficult to read the flashbacks to Victoria's relationship with the professor? How did you react to his suggestions to leave Texas and abandon everything she knows or the use of the violence and rape to dominate Victoria?

6. Did you expect Victoria to attempt suicide? What was your reaction to that scene? Though she felt trapped, what were some of the other options she had beside suicide to get out of the relationship?

7. The story's main theme is about abusive relationships, but what are some of the other motifs in the book? How do these ideas interact with abuse?

8. What were your first impressions of the recovery center, Serenity Now? Did you expect there to be a continuation of narrative drama or were you ready for Victoria to heal and begin to see a resolution?

9. What were some of the signs, both verbal and physical, that Liam would become not only possessive, but also abusive? Why do you think Victoria missed or ignored these signs?

10. Victoria had to learn multiple lessons over the course of the story. What were some of these lessons? Do you think she will carry these lessons with her and continue to learn from them? What lessons will you as the reader take with you?

11. Victoria's family is vital to her recovery. What are some of the key aspects to her relationship with her father, mother, and siblings? Did you expect them to take the actions they did at the end of the book? How did the actions of each character change or enhance their relationship with Victoria?

12. A large emphasis is placed on Victoria's trips home to Texas. Why do you think these trips are so important to her? Does Victoria act differently once she is home? Why or why not?

13. Did Liam's death surprise you? If you had been in Victoria's shoes, how do you think you would have reacted? If you had been in Victoria's mother's position, what actions would you have taken?

14. How did this book change your perception or understanding of abusive relationships? What did you learn from Victoria's story of abuse and recovery that you will remember long after reading?

15. In the final chapter of the book, we learn where everyone is today and how they are doing. Do you think everyone's story ended happily or were some still working towards happiness? Why or why not? Is it okay to need to work on your happiness?

AUTHOR Q & A

Q: **What was your inspiration for writing this story?**

A: I know several women who were abused by sexual predators. While I do not practice criminal law, as an attorney, I was involved in bringing one such predator to something akin to justice. I always wanted to tell a story of these men—because most don't look or act like monsters. They can be family, friends . . . anyone. I want people to understand this.

Q: **How did you develop the flawed, yet compelling character of Victoria?**

A: I knew Victoria would have a somewhat tragic life. I felt that from the beginning, but I also knew she was a survivor. Initially, I didn't want her to be involved in a second abusive relationship, but the story pushed me that way.

Perhaps is was to show that growth sometimes comes at grave costs.

Q: **Are you working on another book now that this book is published? If so, are there any details or insights you can give into your next book?**

A: Yes, I'm working on another story of survival, but in this case, it is based on a true case I handled when I was just out of law school. It involves a young boy who is unexpectedly orphaned, uprooted, and thrust aside . . . but yet he grows into a kind and gentle man who receives an unusual gift.

Q: **Are there any characters that you particularly identify with? What characters did you enjoy developing and writing the most?**

A: Victoria's mom is most like me. I love to have all my children home with all the noise and chaos. I love big family meals and cooking with whomever is willing to help. Having my kitchen full of people, even the little ones, makes me smile. Family is everything to me, and I, like Carolyn, would do anything to protect my children.

I did enjoy Victoria as a character. In a way, she developed herself, especially after her college experience. I was surprised by many of her actions and attributes. She told her story.

Q: **Both the professor and Liam are twisted and disturbing people. Was it difficult or uncomfortable to write such dark characters?**

A: Surprisingly no. I thought it would be, and I struggled with the more violent scenes. But, in the end, they had to speak up to show the true nature of predators.

Q: **What scenes did you enjoy writing the most? What scenes did you find challenging to write?**

A: I can't say any one scene was more challenging than the other nor can I say anyone scene was more enjoyable to write. The characters just took themselves where they wanted to go, which I'm sure sounds strange, but that's the way it felt.

Q: **As you were writing, were you ever surprised by where the story went or some of the decisions a character made? If so, what were these moments and how did you handle the changes to the story you had planned?**

A: Yes, I was very surprised Victoria had the relationship with Liam. I though she and the professor would meet up again. I expected a totally different ending. But, as I said, the characters moved me where they wanted me.

Q: **What were the biggest challenges in writing this story? How did you overcome these challenges?**

A: The biggest challenge was to believe I could write this story. I've tried many times and could never get past a few sentences. About two years ago, this line that opens the book, "Sometimes, she doesn't know the difference between self-loathing and self-pity. They feel so much alike. Both dark. Both cold. Both alone. But they aren't alike. You can keep moving through self-pity. But not with self-loathing," just came to mind. Those words seemed to start the journey to completion. I just knew I would finish.

Q: **Do you have a particular method for writing, such writing at a certain time or location, or always having a cup of coffee or tea? Did you ever face writer's block? What tactics did use to push past it?**

A: I'm a very focused, sporadic writer. I will write four chapters, not getting up for hours and then go days without writing another word. In the interim, below the surface, my mind is working on the next part of the book, the article, whatever the piece may be. When my mind is ready, I start writing again. Maybe the in-between times are a kind of writer's block, but it hasn't ever felt that way or worried me. I just let time work it out.

Q: **Are there any tips and tricks that you developed to help your writing that you would like to share with aspiring authors? Did you receive any advice while writing that was impactful or helpful that you would like to pass on to others?**

A: I don't think I'm qualified to offer much in the way of tips. I've been writing for most of my life, and this book is the first I am willing to share. If I have any advice, it would be to just keep writing . . . if for no one else but yourself and then wait and see what happens.

Q: **Are there any books, podcasts, or other resources you can recommend for women or men who may be in an abusive situation? What about resources for those in crisis to the point of suicide?**

A: One of the first books I read that resonated with me was *Codependent No More* by Melody Beattie. I have given away many copies of this book to people in difficult if not abusive relationships. Another equally profound book for me is *When Bad Things Happen to Good People* by Harold S. Kushner. These two books sum up for me the how of bad relationships and the understanding of cruelty in the world. At the end of the book, I have also included a list of materials as well as information on groups that offer help and guidance to those in life altering situations like those described in the book. It is my prayer that at least one person seeks care and refuge from this book or those resources. One person makes it more than worth the effort.

IF YOU NEED HELP

National Domestic Violence Hotline, 800-799-SAFE (7233)

National Sexual Violence Resource Center, 877-739-3895

Crisis Text Line, Text Home to 741741 to connect with a
Crisis Counselor

National Suicide Prevention Lifeline, 800-273-8255

RAINN, Rape Abuse and Incest National Network,
800-656-HOPE

Loveisrespect (Dating Abuse Helpline), 1-866-331-9471 or
Text loveis to 22522

NOMORE.org, this website provides the following:

- Links to National Helpline for Male Survivors of Sexual Abuse and Assault
- Link to Find Local Rape and Crisis Counseling
- Link to Find Domestic Violence Services

Further Reading

- *Codependent No More: How to Stop Controlling Others and Start Caring for Yourself* by Melody Beattie
- *When Bad Things Happen to Good People* by Harold S. Kushner

ABOUT THE AUTHOR

Rhonda Graff Jolley lives in a small town in South Texas. She is a graduate of the University of Texas at Austin and St. Mary's University School of Law. She has practiced law many years in all areas of the state of Texas. She has four children, four children-in-law, and four grandchildren